# BEST AND FAIREST

## Henry Johnston

Valentine
Press

First published in 2015 by Valentine Press



Valentine Press
P.O. Box 527,
Bellingen NSW 2454
www.valentinepress.com.au

National Library of Australia
Cataloguing-in-Publication entry:
Creator:             Henry Johnston 1951, author
Title:               Best and Fairest
ISBN:                9780994224453 (paperback)
Subjects:
Rugby League football – New South Wales –Sydney –
                     Fiction
Rugby football teams – New South Wales –Sydney –
                     Fiction.
Nineteen-sixties – Fiction.
Sydney (N.S.W.) – Social life and customs – 20th century –
                     Fiction.
Australia – Social life and customs – 20th century – Fiction.
Dewey Number:   A283.4

Front Cover photograph by Geoff Kleem.  Rough clay trophy sculpted by Joe Purtle

Dedicated to Frank Hyde, the voice of Rugby League, and Laurie Nicolls' ghost, shadow boxing along the roads and streets of Rozelle and Balmain one night in 2005.

# Foreword

I first met Henry Johnston while working on a small shipping newspaper, twenty years ago. After a week it was as if I had known him all my life. I reckon that's because he represents an archetype: that of an expansive, genial, and perpetually curious man who loves a drink, a good laugh, and importantly, a decent conversation. In other words, a Sydneysider; like an inner city neighbour where people still live close together, or perhaps the local butcher down the street.

Here is the rub. Not today's butcher, who is angry, anxious and miserable, always looking over his shoulder as the giant supermarkets all around take his livelihood. Henry, or rather Harry, as he is known, is a man of yesteryear, seemingly ripped out of the tough, yet intimate past of Sydney's tribally cohesive communities, to stand in the twenty-first century somewhat bewildered and lost.

*Best and Fairest* is a reverie for the forties, fifties, and sixties merging into a discontinuous narrative of more or less familiar names and places, brands, habits and routines of a Sydney and a people now almost extinct. Indeed, most are dead, and the rest of us who have lived on have replaced ourselves four or five times over – if the research that we completely renew our body cells every seven to ten years is to be believed.

Like a denizen of a city of days gone by, where people walked and caught trams, not drove, Harry is a creature of perambulatory habit to the nth degree, with the tightly circumscribed territory of a domestic cat.

When we worked together in the city, he would always make a beeline for his favourite coffee shop at precisely the same time every day, and, at lunchtime, the same noodle shop under David Jones. A variance from the routine seemed to somehow unsettle him, but being welcomed by a host of an establishment like a friend, calling out his name, was always a joy.

To describe Harry as tribal is not, in any way, an insult. It is the happy truth. When he lobbed here from Birmingham, UK, via Townsville, his family moved to Sydney's inner-west and that is where he still is today, 55 years later; his tribal loyalties undiminished. That includes Rugby League.

And, hence this novella of an inner city Sydney – with its golden facades of sandstone once hand hewn by men in leather aprons – peopled by factory toilers, punters, small time crooks and bookies; all characters just like himself.

In Stanley Kubrick's film, *The Shining*, the antihero, Jack Torrance, an alcoholic writer (played by Jack Nicholson) is drawn in by the bartender – one of a retinue of ghostly ectoplasms of a hotel's colourful if unsavoury past. Eventually, Torrance steps out of his reality and into the former times.

Harry is doing something similar. He has conjured a living past out of his need to be there with it, because, for all its faults, it was good.

**Jack Rozycki**
**28 August 2015**

# Preface

My son, an avid Bulldogs supporter, believes Rugby League is Sydney's dirty little secret, a game that runs counter to the aspirations of average Sydneysiders. I agree to a point. We live in one of the world's great, global metropolises, and seek to impress international guests with delightful vistas of the harbour before enjoying a languid lunch on the foreshore, or at a beachside bistro. And yet, as March approaches, we pay more attention to the small details of our communities. Sydney becomes Marrickville or Leichhardt or Cronulla, or Parramatta, Ashfield, Hurlstone Park, Manly, Canterbury or Forest Lodge, Redfern, Pagewood or La Perouse. The list is long. I doubt a tourist would recognise these names as 'Sydney', but they are the essence of social groupings where we coalesce into winter tribes keen to celebrate rituals passed from fathers, grandmothers and great grandparents. Spend any Sunday afternoon in July on the streets circling Kogarah Oval, and marvel at streams of men, women and children wearing ill-fitting white shirts with a red V slashed on the front. Their pride is palpable. Now walk the eerie green sward of Callan Park toward Leichhardt Oval on a similar Sunday, and count the orange and black jerseys. Tell me you don't sense the presence of the ghosts of hundreds of thousands of men and women who trod the same streets from the early 1900s through the decades to the present day. These winter rites are repeated across Sydney, north to Newcastle, south to Wollongong, west to Penrith and in rural towns and cities across the length and breadth of New South Wales.

In 2014, thousands of supporters wept after the South Sydney Rabbitohs won a grand final that bore a remarkable similarity to a victory of forty-three years earlier. Perry Keyes captures the mood of that great 1970s win in his song, *The Day John Sattler Broke His Jaw*.

Premier Neville Wran famously said Balmain boys don't cry, but in 2005 my community of Rozelle erupted in joyous revelry when Wests Tigers won the pennant. And yet, despite the emotion of a Rugby League grand final, it remains a game every bit as tough and brutal as depicted in the British film *This Sporting Life*, based on the eponymous novel by David Storey.

While State of Origin has all but eclipsed the Kangaroos/England tour, Rugby League test matches played in the bleak north counties remain a last great tie to the traditions of the British Empire.

I wrote the first draft of *Best and Fairest* in the mid-1990s, convinced Rugby League would not survive the grasp of an international corporation, but the game defied and defeated the juggernaut, adopted its innovations, and became better, faster, fairer.

After South Sydney's remarkable 2014 win, my friend John Conomos, urged me to redraft the manuscript, which I revised into its present form.

As a work of fiction, the novella relies on hundreds of Sydney anecdotes from its past. While they impart pace and structure, they are not historically accurate. *Best and Fairest* is a portrait of Sydney as glimpsed through the lens of an inverted telescope. The principal narrative is the team's football season; however some events occur before and after this time line.

In telling these stories I do not ascribe wrongdoing, nor do I impugn the reputation nor character of any person, living or dead.

I acknowledge the traditional owners of the land about which I have written, especially the

Eora, Gadigal and Dharruk nations. I pay my respects to their elders past, present and future, and offer tribute to Australian Aboriginal men and women, who with extraordinary grace and sensitivity welcomed me to *their* country.

**Henry Johnston**

# CONTENTS

# The Darlington Under Fourteen All Stars

Number Six, **Walter Sugden** (Captain and five eighth)

Number Seven, **Quentin Gallagher** (Halfback)

Number Eight, **Neil Davidson** (Prop)

Number Nine, **Cyril Smyth** (Hooker)

Number Ten, **Ken Casey** (Prop)

Number Eleven, **Anthony Moroney** (Second row)

Number Twelve, **John Flood** (Second row)

Number Thirteen, **Enzo Cuda** (Lock forward)

Number Five, **Declan Bennett** (Left wing)

Number Four, **Peter Tregonning** (Left centre)

Number Three, **Mark Tregonning** (Right centre)

Number Two, **Billy Bomer** (Right wing)

Number One, **Chris Robertson** (Vice-captain and fullback)

**Jimmy Bomer** (Coach)

**Vincent Vansittart** (Reserve)

# Chapter One
# Shadows

I treasure simple experiences; a summer sky starched and faded to cornflower blue, or the relief of a southerly buster cooling the worst of the day's heat. I celebrate October's purple, dazzling jacarandas, and marvel at the tenacity of an insistent bullfrog, croaking for a mate in the depths of an overflowing, rusted iron tub. And as I consider these gossamer things, I ponder the ineffable changes in my life.

Yesterday, as the sun's arc shifted higher, I glimpsed a lifelong companion: my shadow, lockstep in front, constant over my shoulder, fluid by left and right. And though I am now stooped, my shadow showed a self much as it was, when as a child I first recognised its existence.

There are times when other shadows join my wandering. I see their faces, and conjure memories of forgotten conversations. I hear the phantom clatter of ball-bearing wheels rasping and screeching the underside of a rickety billy cart down the Darlington back streets. A constant, tedious scrape means slow times, but frequent, measured silences spell an increase of sales of the inky afternoon tabloids, snatched by scurrying men, dashing for the 5.10pm steamer to Parramatta or Hurstville.

Six o'clock and the streets belong once more to Darlington's denizens, coughing up the dust and coal smoke coiling from the cooling Eveleigh boilers, drifting the length of Abercrombie Street to Broadway and Central Railway Station, before settling close by the garment alleys of Surry Hills.

A cascading toxic pink patina stains that late March dusk of long ago.

Succulent steam rises from a thousand meaty dinner pies, crusty crisp and golden, cooking in four room cottages in Golden Grove and Camperdown. Working men roll up cuff-less sleeves, casting furrowed glances at enticing headlines, before turning to the back page sports news, with appetites whetted by the succulent aroma, and the anticipation of the first weekend round of football

But no hot pie for Darlington's aspiring under fourteens. Cold Devon sandwiches churn butterflies in thirteen nervous stomachs, for this year a victorious schoolboy state championship side tours England with the Kangaroos. Outstanding players dream the unimaginable; recruitment by the South Sydney Rabbitohs or the Newtown Blue Bags.

The first Monday of autumn. The premiere training session of the season. A chilly night when languid skills sharpened at the summer crease, and honed in explosive games of tip football on Coogee Beach, mean nothing if a member of last year's "thirteens" fail their bid for selection.

Acceptance in the under fourteen squad offers the chance of a career beyond the tool sheds and factories. The fourteenth year tolls childhood's passing, and entry to the harsh, glittering world of adults.

Nominal captain Walter Sugden dons a hard-won training uniform, comprising an old Bankstown jersey, and white patched shorts. A pair of long, green and gold socks signals first grade ambitions. Walter walks with a skipper's modesty, a gait redolent of dignity in victory, pluckiness in defeat.

The previous year the victorious Darlington under thirteens won a rugged grand final against their old rivals. As tradition demanded, the captains swapped jerseys with each other. At the final whistle, Walter exchanged his shirt with the toughest fullback he had ever played, a brooding brown-eyed kid who in a promise-filled future, became the 24ᵗʰ Prime Minister of Australia.

Every Saturday morning in a ritual of bravado, Walter pummels the fast ball at the local Police Boys Club. Boxing lessons develop speed and agility, and sharpen the knack of reading an opponent's strategy. Darlington men reckon Walter this year's choice for Best and Fairest, and in a few years, a first grade certainty.

Money is scarce in the Sugden household. And to pay his keep, each workday afternoon Walter hauls the billy cart, filled with late extra editions. He detests the moniker 'paper boy', and fights fist and boot a gang of fifth-formers who tease him with the epithet, and often beat him bloody in the dingy, dangerous lanes of Golden Grove.

The owner of Walter's paper run, Murray Dwyer, risks most of the newsagency takings with the local starting price bookmaker. Each day from 10.00am to 3.00pm, Murray studies the turf guide, analysing the form of every horse listed to race at Randwick, Canterbury, or Warwick Farm. For relief, he thumbs the latest editions of *Men Only* magazine, ogling the bosomy models.

Murray knows his customers' secrets, and keeps book on local scandals, trading information to the coppers when down a few quid. By 5.30pm each weekday, he divvies the deeners, draws the shutters, locks the newsagency and sprints to the Golden Grove Hotel, thirsty for a boisterous schooner amid the mayhem of the six o'clock swill.

One of his pastimes remains a murderous secret. Each summer weekend Murray prowls the remote sand hills of Cronulla's Wanda Beach, spying on boys dallying with their girlfriends. But he seeks lone girls sunbathing topless, and on one fateful Sunday, spent hours watching two beautiful young women. Neither saw him approach.

Walter's father Francis Xavier Sugden – Frankie to his mates – posts the starting price at the Golden Grove Hotel. Frankie's business partner, broken-nosed Police Sergeant Mick Vaughan, ensures fair policing of the book.

Frankie and Murray loathe one another. Frankie calls Murray a mongrel for his condescension to local workers, and despises his support of the chamber of commerce, his membership of the Master Carpenters' Guild, and his crony gang of toady factory managers. Yet without hesitation, Frankie takes Murray's bets, paying out on a win, or touching his nose when a nag comes in last.

The paper seller, aspiring football star and altar boy at St Gloria's unwittingly maintained a sulky peace between his father and Murray Dwyer, but on this distant, smoky autumn Monday night, at the end of the Age of Steam, the Bug struts out of his parents' terrace house, day-dreaming of running onto the Sydney Cricket Ground, as captain and five eighth.

# Chapter Two
# Henson Park

The Davidson family hailed from ancient Yorkshire, and honoured Rugby League with the motto *Defy and Defend,* a dour creed popular in Kingston-upon-Hull, and article of faith of generations of the Davidson family kith and kin. As with most citizens born in the home town of William Wilberforce, the Davidsons chose defiance of the master, and defence of the defenceless.

Graeme Davidson trained as a shipwright, but the appeal of warm, blue antipodean skies tempered centuries of loyalty to King and Country.

Graeme and wife Doris joined the post-war vanguard of English migrants to Australia. Twelve years on, and with an accent as thick as the Hull River, Graeme helped build the destroyer HMAS *Voyager,* bifurcated by HMAS *Melbourne* in Australia's worst peacetime maritime disaster.

Doris, Graeme and their three children, settled on a two up, two down in Darlington, a bone-rattling thirty-minute tram ride from Cockatoo Island.

The family adopted the Rabbitohs of South Sydney, named for the sellers of fresh rabbit carcasses carried on long, thin poles. Now on the eve of a new football season, Graeme roars at eldest boy Neil, scrum prop, to stop scuffing his younger brother. Neil blusters into the parlour, but before speaking, the old man slips him a shilling.

"Tram fare, boy. Mind you don't spend it all, and back sharpish in time for homework." A dry-throated Neil kisses his father's cheek, throws a pair of patched togs into a duffle bag, and shuffles into the chilly twilight.

The thirteen aspirants, accompanied by their trainer, converge at a Broadway tram stop and unleash a good-humoured bout of shoving, jostling, shaping-up and shouting over one another.

Chris Robertson, a gangling kid from Forest Lodge, sports the fullback's number one. Tony Moroney swipes at the halfback Quentin Gallagher, who darts as a blowfly. The wingers, sullen, skinny cousins from Redfern stand apart, shifting from foot to foot. Billy Bomer generally bests his cousin Declan Bennet, who runs a shade slower, courtesy of cigarettes smoked before and after training.

Lock Enzo Cuda looms large beneath the dim tram stop light. Thirteen-year-old Enzo stands 5'9" and shaves with a cut-throat razor. Each morning before school Enzo hauls potatoes at his father's stall in Paddy's Markets, and carries his birth certificate to every match as proof of age.

Rimless glasses frame the freckled face of hooker Cyril Smyth, whose piston feet lash the scrum. Cyril's bony elbows bite into the shoulders of the two props, Neil Davidson and big boy, Kenny Casey. A well-aimed shoulder charge by big Ken can flatten an opponent, but a fondness for meat pies renders him a slowcoach. Centres, the Tregonning twins Mark and Peter, push and shove one another.

As dusk fades to night, the group board a tram for Henson Park, a bleak, windswept paddock, circled by a bicycle track, and dominated by the concrete King George V stand. Henson Park, is loathed as the worst ground in the competition, and boasts a notorious shin-scraping turf.

The mob crowds the dressing room, pulls on mothball-scented togs amid yips and tense banter, but the din drops to a murmur as Billy's father and coach, Jimmy Bomer, threatens a brutal workout. Jimmy promises a backhander to anyone who complains, or doesn't finish the training. Not a word is spoken.

"Where's bloody Declan?" Jimmy sprays furious spittle towards Billy.

"Dunno."

"What do mean 'you don't know'? Go and get him, and tell him if I smell those friggin' smokes, I'll beat his bloody hide."

Nervous sniggers break the silence.

"Laps, now," Jimmy booms. Billy, first through the gate, and the puffing Declan lurking outside, hit the turf with a gust of speed. Jimmy shakes his head.

"Bloody smokes will kill ya," yells Declan.

By 8.30pm a pain-wracked group waits for the last tram to Darlington. The otherwise jovial Kenny Casey sits silent, sore and sullen, pondering a warning by the coach to trim weight or leave.

A quarter past nine. Neil places the key into the front door of his home a few blocks from Wattle Street.

"Shower, homework and bed," but mute with fatigue, Neil nods toward his father, limps upstairs, and falls asleep in his clothes.

As stillness settles around the house, on silent tiptoe Graeme enters Neil's room, unravels tangled muddy boot laces, brushes matted hair from his son's forehead, drapes blanket across bed and ushers in the night with a sharp tug of the light-switch cord. Then, hands outstretched and patting the darkness, he wide-eyed walks to the soft snore, sonorous bedroom, turns down the coverlet and embraces Doris, adrift in warm, dreamless slumber.

# Chapter Three
# Moon tree

Ernest John Tregonning made up for a lack of sporting ability with morbid pride in the prowess of his twin sons. Ernest belted Mark and Peter if they failed to play football to his standard.

Ernie loved to drink, and joined thousands of men consuming the amber fluid as if pure burnished, liquid gold. Pint followed schooner into mouths parched by coal smuts, as drinkers drew breath flavoured by the acrid fumes of ready-rubbed, shag tobacco. Darlington public houses opened early to slake the thirst of tired night shift workers, sub-editors, ambulance drivers, or those driven mad with *delirium tremens*. The barmen drew off a steady, icy stream till lunch, and on to the deadly hour of the six o'clock swill. At four thirty, as steam whistles blew shift change, a race began to favoured pubs dotted around the Eveleigh rail yards. By 5.00pm, shouting, grimy men, Ernie among them, near drank bars dry before red-faced publicans locked the doors on the stroke of six o'clock.

Sydney's largest brewery belched a reeking, meady mist into the sooty Broadway air. Hefty beer carts pulled by giant, straining teams of Clydesdales, delivered thousands of kegs across the city, every day of every working week.

Stokers firing locomotive boilers dreamt of holidays by the sea, winning the Sydney Opera House Lottery, or scoring a big pay-out on a horse. These silent recurring fantasies transported them from the barren freight yards, but the reality of a Saturday trip to Royal Randwick lay beyond the means of most families. A long, return tram journey proved too expensive just to watch dad lose his shirt on a balmy Saturday afternoon.

Each alternate Wednesday, Ernie gambled on race meetings at Canterbury or Rosehill, parleying a starting price with Frankie Sugden. Ernie and his fellow punters knew not to drink too much, and keep the noise to a minimum, for by so doing they avoided a beating by the coppers cruising the Darlington streets in the Black Maria. The boys in blue ensured tardy punters settled up with Frankie. A loser had the choice of a trip to the pawn shops on Oxford Street, or a kicking. The coppers' motto was, 'fair is fair, so cop it sweet'.

At the midpoint of the previous successful under thirteens year, Ernie argued with the school sports master over Enzo's selection. The giant Italian finished the season most improved, but the twins whined to their father, saying Enzo scored a try deemed a sitter for Peter. The spat concluded when the school principal told Mr. Tregonning hundreds of so called 'wog' children now formed a constituent part of the life of the nation. Later that night elder twin Peter endured a sharp beating, a common experience on days Ernie did not drink to stupefaction.

Marlene Tregonning endured the worst of her husband's violence in silence. Infrequent, drunken, amorous advances meant a bloody beating when she refused Ernie's demand for sex.

Thirty-three-year-old Marlene counted the passing of grey, interminable days. She married the handsome Ernest at age 20, and set to work as his private valet and nursemaid to her twins. As the boys grew, and as Ernie's violence became more frequent, Marlene persuaded a doctor to prescribe Pethidine to ease persistent gynaecological pain, caused by near fatal labour. Though the drug helped relieve the dull ache of the beatings, it induced breathless sleep, and grotesque nightmares. Marlene dreamt a duo of slithering black snakes tasted the air with forked tongues as they coiled amid the long grass by the choko-strewn privy. On another fitful night she floated above her bed, watching her motionless image standing at the bottom of a crater on the moon, choking for air and clutching her throat as a shower of leaves fell from the knotty branches of a giant, white tree.

On Tuesdays, Marlene volunteered at the St. Gloria's tuck shop. Glad for the company of other women, the gossip and the hustle, she glanced at the senior boys, and had no sense of the sparkle in her eyes as she sold the luncheon produce. Pursed lips greeted the twins' arrival in the shop, for Marlene determined neither son would enjoy the preferential service of extra sauce on Mark's pie or a larger cream bun for Peter. The other women did not notice Marlene's steely gaze, and as always the twins ignored their mother.

The Tregonning family lived in a neat three-bedroom terrace in Paints Lane, Darlington, adjacent to City Road. At a later time, a nearby location earned the nickname the Tin Sheds, and became a venue for print-making of world renown. Ernie believed the inexpensive lease-back arrangement would last a lifetime, but within a few years, entire streets, which housed close-knit families, disappeared from the road maps, swallowed by the juggernaut needs of Sydney University.

The site of the city's grand academy of the Victorian era demanded extra space. The bulldozers moved in and flattened swathes of the boroughs of Darlington, Golden Grove and Camperdown to satisfy the needs of a growing student populace and their tutors.

Many of the streets and laneways where the under fourteens grew, now lie buried beneath bland faculty architecture, while a few intact houses are restored according to the tastes of the academic gentry.

During the war, Petty Officer Tregonning served as quartermaster in the naval catering corps. The sole action Ernie witnessed was a riot among thirty drunken mates and terrified Aboriginals at Nowra on the New South Wales South Coast.

Ernie valorised Anzac Day, and each year regaled his mates with the story of the Japanese midget submarine that sank HMAS *Kuttabul*. Ernie's pals knew he missed the train from Nowra on the day war came to Sydney, but each committed warrior of the rear kept shtum as

Ernie sank schooner after schooner, and shot a hundred Japanese.

On the night of a wet Anzac Day, after a raucous binge with his navy mates, Ernie stumbled home to what he believed a frigid, conjugal bed. He told the prosecutor in Central Street Local Court he became enraged when he caught his wife dallying with another man. Marlene survived several hammer blows to her face and head, but vowed to the judge her husband had not attempted to kill her, describing her attacker as a smiling youth with moonlit, silver hair, who held the bough of a leafless tree above her. The fantastic story kept court reporters speculating for the duration of the trial. One front page headline read, 'attempted manslaughter by moonlight' but the author did not bother to check the phase of the moon, which, on this terrible, violent night, was new.

Navy comrades passed the hat around for a fund to help the Tregonning family, but by night's end Ernie's mates spent the takings at an almighty booze up in the Marrickville Returned Services League Club.

Marlene Tregonning went blind during an eighteen-month stay in Odyssey House, trying to quell her Pethidine addiction. A massive stroke paralysed the left quadrant of her body, and Mark and Peter agreed with a social worker to admit their mother to a nursing home.

Years after, neither twin attended Marlene's funeral, remaining on duty at the Twin Palms Motel in Port Macquarie which they bought with the proceeds of an *ex gratia* payment from the New South Wales Government as recompense for their father's criminality.

Ernie signed his bail papers at Cooma prison on his sixtieth birthday. When he arrived at Central Railway Station, a jailhouse preference for the company of catamites led him to a Turkish steam bath near the intersection of Commonwealth and Oxford Streets, Surry Hills.

Ernest John Tregonning, former fitter and turner in the car trade in Zetland, died in the early 1980s from a mysterious disease which triggered rapid pulmonary pneumonia. During the last seventy-two hours of life, deep red sarcoma blotches disfigured his papery, yellowing skin. A puzzled doctor at St Vincent's Hospital speculated on his patient's history as a smoker. But of the millions of men and women who inhaled the fumes of Ardath, Woodbine, Rothmans and hundreds of other brands of

cigarettes, Ernie Tregonning was one of the few
who did not smoke.

# Chapter Four
# Workers' Paradise

Jovial ruddy faced Kenny Casey tried hard at sport, but star status remained elusive. Ken loafed in class, yet somehow managed to score in the top five per cent. And although teachers and school mates admired the big, good-natured adolescent, few paid him genuine attention. Not one schoolmate knew of Ken's talent as a boy soprano, a fact he was happy to keep secret. The angelic voice broke during the under fourteen year, bestowing the lifelong gift of a mellifluous tenor timbre.

Éamon, Ken's father, bore the physique of a boxer, honed from years of labouring. In the late 1950s Éamon, a skilled rigger, signed on to a building job at Bennelong Point, where he worked until the day Queen Elizabeth II opened the Sydney Opera House.

Éamon retired to a happy life of gardening and fine music. His favourite opera, *Pagliacci,* made him cry when his son dedicated his debut performance of Leoncavallo's sad clown to his father in the Opera House Theatre Éamon helped build.

But Casey senior did not fit the stereotype of the sentimental Irishman. At thirteen he ran messages for the IRA in County Cork, and at fifteen studied the *Communist Manifesto* on a train trip to Leningrad in the year Josef Stalin murdered Sergei Kirov, the city's Communist Party boss.

The stopover in the Workers' Paradise hardened into full party membership, and Éamon became a softly-spoken evangelist of the Communist Internationale. He slipped unnoticed into Australia at war's end, but his politics attracted the attention of ASIO during the dark years of a world filled with wandering, shell-shocked refugees. Éamon's talent for honeyed oratory, plus a faculty for organisation, helped defeat Robert Menzies' anti-communist referendum.

The closest Éamon came to a heart attack occurred during a night at the cinema. Flickering on the black and white Movietone newsreels, lurched the spectral image of Vladimir Petrov, struggling with a KGB emissary, a thick-set moustached man and personal bodyguard of Comrade Vyacheslav Molotov. In the 1920s, this

KGB agent and Éamon toasted Red victories during long, drunken nights in the Smolny Institute. Now, sitting with his family in the back row of the mock velvet plush of the Barclay Cinema, Éamon watched the bodyguard compel a reluctant Petrov to return to the Workers' Paradise.

Éamon believed culture the great reward of political struggle, and peace its dividend. The personification of his beliefs came on a sultry Sydney summer's day, when a giant, black American man performed for Sydney Opera House workers and their families.

Paul Robeson sang slave songs, work chants, madrigals of revolution, hope and sadness, and ended the concert with a medley from *Porgy and Bess*. Ken Casey, boy tenor, took up the melody of *Summertime*, harmonising with Robeson to the end. The great man applauded Ken, and signed a dedication to the Casey family on the dust cover of one of Éamon's 78 rpm records. The framed autograph hangs to this day in the Sydney Opera House Green Room.

# Chapter Five
# On the Susso

This night, in the bleak empty expanse of Henson Park, football coach Jimmy Bomer threatened Ken Casey with an abrupt end to his last shot for a position in the under fourteens.

But during the first fourteen years of *his* life, Jimmy Bomer wandered a twilight world where skin colour marked a person as either half, or quarter caste.

Born during the Great Depression in a blacks' camp on the fringes of Walgett, Jimmy passed a bewildered childhood, lost to the black man's Dreaming, and a fugitive of white fella law.

Jimmy's family were among the first rural blacks to shift to Redfern. He grew up in a sequence of terraced houses in the bleak confines of Eveleigh Street, and joined hundreds of children eating watery gruel at a soup kitchen on the corner of Abercrombie Street and Broadway and run by well-meaning Christians.

During the summer, Jimmy cadged rides on the Manly ferry and spent the day diving for coins. Mesmerised day trippers watched the shivering brown kid plunge off the massive wharf crossbeams, arrowing through the water and back to the surface, holding a penny or a shilling coin.

With mates at his heels, Jimmy jumped the running boards of industrial trams hauling bulk goods through the sleeping city streets. He collected and sold manure, and touted for fares for the hansom cab drivers on Eddy Avenue at Central Railway. Jimmy's mother buried tins of food in the backyard during the worst days of the Depression. The Susso – sustenance – inspectors enforced the same allocation for everyone by confiscating excess food, a practice Jimmy thought strange, especially as the display windows of the Buckingham's and Snows' emporia brimmed with stock.

On Saturday nights, Jimmy and his older cousins visited local pubs to stock family parties with dozens of 'two sips' – sample bottles of beer.

An old uncle pulled out a battered guitar and sang bush ballads and popular tunes. On Sunday morning, Jimmy and the entire Bomer clan walked to Redfern Oval to barrack at the junior

Rugby League games. There, among friends and relatives, they forgot tedium and poverty for a few happy hours.

Parents took pride in the football courage of their children, but by late afternoon the women came together, and began to cry to their aunties and sisters about lost brown skin babies, taken to service in big houses in Cootamundra, Parramatta, Coonamble and other country settlements with musical, Aboriginal names. By day's end, the clans remembered the old times in country, and the casual savagery of the mongrel coppers.

In the last football season before the outbreak of war, a trainload of Bomer relatives made the bone-breaking trip from Walgett to Sydney for a shambolic three-day footy comp. The victors returned with a trophy sculpted from red clay, crafted on the freezing shores of Lake Cargelligo. Despite overwhelming problems of organisation, the coaches arranged a return contest for the following season.

After Prime Minister Menzies declared war in unison with Great Britain, both coaches joined the AIF. One died at the Fall of Singapore, the other blinded by an exploding hand grenade during a skirmish near Lae. Aboriginality meant pay far below the wages of white servicemen, and their service ignored by the Returned Services League.

But Aboriginal football associations grew apace after war's end. Scores of men competing in first grade league competitions in Queensland and New South Wales doubled-up for Koori country knockouts, similar to the tournaments Jimmy Bomer played as a youth.

Each weekend Jimmy's son Billy and his nephew Declan kicked the ball around with the Redfern Blacks. Both boys remained non-committal about playing with a Walgett team in a country grand final. Jimmy understood the significance of both competitions for the cousins, so if the boys wouldn't play football in rural Walgett, Jimmy planned to bring the bush to them.

# Chapter Six
# Just For Fun

The Reverend Brothers Harlan and Eugene lived by the motto, *give me the boy and I'll show you the man*. As St Gloria's predominant teachers, their innate practicality tempered idealism.

Before the war, Harlan cut sugar cane near Mackay in Queensland, and Eugene taught physical education in the Australian Army. Both men fulfilled their vows with a rough and tumble piety. School was life, football its locus. Neither brooked cheek from man nor boy, and beating sense into shirkers sprang from a simple commitment to an elementary set of principles: educate poor children, strengthen their bodies, see them into the world, and prepare for next year's intake. The formula remained unaltered for thirty years. Their philosophy assumed most of their charges would graduate to a life of hard, physical work, yet both fretted over the exceptions; the bright students studying for the Intermediate Certificate, and the exceptional few who remained an extra couple of years, cramming for the Leaving Certificate.

An education system built on the model of the English greater public schools provided a safety valve for this intelligent minority, but the cost to struggling parents oft times proved ruinous. Bursaries provided one or two of this small band the opportunity of tertiary education. When safely ensconced with other colleagues studying on a Commonwealth Scholarship, or on the Colombo Plan, the intelligent progeny of the poor were moulded into replicas of their benefactors. But many local undergraduates, subsidised by the bursary system, chose to read Marx and Engels alongside their Colombo Plan comrades. Thus at war's end, revolution spread throughout the remnants of the British Empire, while young, headstrong Australians joined sundry political parties, and infiltrated the academic system which coached them.

The secular creed of sporting success spurred Harlan and Eugene to win a state championship for the school. Both men sensed the victorious potential of the new fourteens side. Despite a cloistered life, each understood the challenges of this seminal year. For those on the cusp of adulthood, inborn innocence would be a hallmark of life — physical strength tempered by compassion — but for others, the vagaries of puberty would destroy any lingering semblance of childhood idealism. Many young heads would turn by the end of this year, with the majority destined to emulate their fathers' lives. A handful yearned for a promising future, and several remained as youths in the guise of manhood, measuring lost adolescence by grey hair, or the spreading paunch of cynicism. Enzo, for example, lived in a man's body, and Ken Casey's voice sounded like a cracked bell, while the remainder grew like swamp weeds. But for this moment in the lives of Brothers Harlan and Eugene, the rabble appeared capable of a triumph worthy of a framed colour photograph which, as time passed, would fade in the musty sunlit silence of the school assembly hall.

Jimmy Bomer persuaded Harlan and Eugene to allow him to take the players to a pre-season training session at North Sydney Oval. Several games would be played against schools from north of the harbour. Jimmy reasoned familiarisation with a foreign ground might improve the chance of coping with away nerves. The Reverend Brothers granted nothing unless they saw a tangible return, and Jimmy's foresight brought the trophy within their grasp.

The boys assembled at the Railway Square tram terminus, clambered aboard a Circular Quay bound 'toast rack', and skylarked all the way to the Rocks where they split into two groups of five and eight for the warm up walk across the Sydney Harbour Bridge.

The band of five fell behind, ambling mute amid the shadows of shuttered houses and derelict bond stores, stretching the length of George Street, north to the Argyle Cut.

Wharf labourers waiting for their shift gang, stared from gloomy pubs. Cobbled flagstones glistened in the sun, as slimy green water trickled from sheer cliffs, nourishing thick moss growing on the flagstone gutters. Stunted Moreton Bay figs peeped out of crevices in the cracked, brittle sandstone.

Quentin Gallagher said razor gangs patrolled the Rocks.

"Where are the others?" Tony asks, but John, Cyril, Quentin and Enzo, remain silent, save for the pinging of their footsteps echoing across the weeping stone archway.

A girl stands in the corner of a laneway across the Argyle Cut. John walks toward her.

"How do you get onto the Harbour Bridge?"

"Go up the flight steps where your mates are standing, and follow the path," she says.

"What's your name?" John does not expect an answer, but with coy, raised eyes, the girl replies, "Pandora."

A querulous man whines from a nearby house, "Who are you talking with Dora?"

"You better go." Her tone coaxes the hairs on the nape of John's neck upright.

"Might see you later?"

Dora whispers, "OK."

"Where and when?" John's cheeks redden.

"Dora!" The man's angry voice ratchets to menacing.

"Saturday."

"Where? Here?"

"Circular Quay. Ten o'clock." Cold streams of sweat trickle the length of John's back. Saliva thickens in his mouth. "Coming." Dora's voice sounds sing-song.

John turns toward his frantic waving friends, and when he looks back over his shoulder for a final glance, Dora is gone. Across the Argyle Cut, Enzo points up the hill toward a group of boys walking in their direction, their height exaggerated by a shaft of sunlight at their back.

"Up here." Quentin darts along a flight of steps. Tony and Cyril follow, but Enzo and John hang back. The first youth grabs Enzo by the collar, but he twists out of the grasp and shoves his fist into the boy's face.

"Piss off!" The hard-faced youth unbuckles a heavy, studded belt.

"We're going mate." Enzo edges up the steep steps.

"Don't come back."

"Sure," John says, and he and Enzo walk further along the incline, then breathless at the top of the stairs, notice their three friends pointing toward a long, inclining footpath snaking through a spinney of steel-grey bridge spars, rising skyward beyond the southern pylon.

"Let's go!" Enzo shouts and the five run at full speed toward the centre of the bridge.

Sydney Harbour folds out in a turquoise coruscation stretching westward to the Blue Mountains. A white passenger steamer, wisps of smoke curling from its funnel, sits moored at Pier One, Walsh Bay. Harbour ferries arrow toward the Bald Rock wharf before veering back into the main stream and steaming west to Gladesville, and the invisible mouth of the Parramatta River. Red rattler trains clatter over the bridge, as streams of cars and trucks speed along adjacent lanes.

As the footpath curves toward an imperceptible crest, the fear-filled gallop slows to walking pace. Trailing fingers trace the strength of innumerable cold, grey rivets. Each youth stares at the glittering water, stealing an occasional backward glance, but the threat has passed.

"How far to the water do you reckon?"

"I'd say five hundred feet, Quentin. You'd be a goner if you jumped." Tony sets his mouth to the cyclone wire and spits, but a gust of wind catches the glob, and flings it back on his cheek. His friends fall over laughing, and as the concrete portals atop the Rocks' stairs disappear, the green, leafy outline of Lavender Bay fills the horizon. North Sydney lies below their tread.

"The rest of the mob's there." Cyril points to a park beneath the northern pylon where a football spirals the length of the turf, in a game of half-hearted tip.

A furious Jimmy hisses, "Where did you lot get to?"

"We looked around, and you were gone."

"Let's go," Jimmy shouts, and the re-united group stroll away from the harbour, past neat

Federation-style cottages, nestling on manicured, quarter-acre blocks. A blend of seaweed and sweet lavender scents the air. Currawongs warble in pale green plane trees planted on bright, storybook streets. Flocks of rosellas skim mansions, hidden behind high, sandstone walls, and set back from roads free of trucks and carts. An arch, festooned with thick neon tubes, spans a main road, welcoming visitors to Luna Park with the sign, *Just for Fun*.

A neat picket fence circles the lush turf of North Sydney Oval. Cabbage palm trees line the path to the dressing sheds, where the players change into their training gear. A pair of stocky men strut across the echoing room; one walks toward Jimmy, the other hangs back making small talk.

"How's it going, Georgie?" a beaming Jimmy affectionately shakes the man's outstretched hand.

"Yeah, good, Jim. This the Darlington mob?" Jimmy places an arm around George, and whistles for attention. The banter drops to a murmur.

"Boys. Meet a pal of mine. Mr George Ambrum arranged for us to come here for practice this afternoon. For those of youse who don't know,

Mr Ambrum plays first grade for the North Sydney Bears." A round of applause resonates off the concrete walls.

"Outside and warm up," but as steel studded boots clatter out of the shed, and onto the springy turf, Jimmy holds Declan and Billy aside.

"I want youse to meet a mate of mine from Queensland. Lionel Morgan."

"How you going, brother." The twang of the outback sings in Lionel's lilting voice.

"Good to put a face to the pictures." The awestruck cousins recognise the great Queensland winger, but neither can manage more than a perfunctory "g'day."

"What positions do youse play?" And as Lionel smiles at George and Jimmy, Declan says "wing."

"Is he fast, Jim?"

"He'll be another Larry Marsh if he stops smoking," Jimmy lightly cuffs Declan over the back of the head.

"Out youse go. I'll be there in a sec." The cousins shake hands with both men and, with puffed chests, clatter on to the pitch.

"So do you reckon you'll get a Test spot this year, Lionel?" Jimmy winks and nudges George in the ribs.

"Be a first for us mob if he does," says George. The three men exchange small talk, and watch the preliminary exercises in silence before bidding one another goodbye.

Jimmy trots on to the field, and shouting sharp instructions, runs with one group, then the other in a game of seven against six. Passes shoot along the back line. Scything tackles stop set moves, followed by crisp play-the-ball, and precise drop kicks. Chris pops six out of six goals, as the team trains as if being watched by a crowd, but thirteen inspired boys from the inner west have North Sydney Oval to themselves.

From 1956 to 1974, George Ambrum played 157 club matches for North Sydney, and represented Australia in two test matches. Lionel Morgan is recognised as the first Aboriginal to play for Australia, competing in two tests and the 1960 Rugby League World Cup.

# Chapter Seven
# In it to win it

"Not an ounce of spare flesh, mate. Not a skerrick in twenty years. I don't drink or smoke." Michael Patrick Vaughan pats his waistline.

"But you are a bugger of a gambler." Frankie Sugden nods to the barmaid for whiskey.

A sergeant in the New South Wales Police, Mick Vaughan gazes the length of the Golden Grove public bar, studying the faces of wizened, spectacled men reading the turf guide, and circling selections for the Saturday race meetings. Mick encountered similar men in country pubs around the Victorian High Country, and in fly-blown towns dotted across the Western Districts of New South Wales.

Born in the flat, brown wheat lands of the Hay Plain, Mick grew up in an endless cycle of rural drudgery. He learnt the gambler's code at two-up games in shearing sheds along the banks of the Murrumbidgee River. On his 18th birthday, Mick watched a travelling show set up the Big Top on the outskirts of a forgotten shit-speck town. Coloured electric lights decorated the tents of the *Headless Lady*, the *Wall of Death*, and *The Strong Man*. Show spruikers enticed the country folk to "have a go, try your luck, be in it to win it." Air rifles thwacked tin targets as a leather thong clattered against the nail of the ever-spinning wheel of fortune, but scores of torn lucky tickets littered the red soil, as the showmen skinned the country folk with disarming ease.

A bass drum pounded for hours before closing time. Ringers, bush cooks and local toughs headed for Jimmy Sharman's boxing tent, keen to go toe-to-toe with broken-nosed pugs. Now and then one might win a stoush, staggering away with a split upper eyelid, and sore head, clutching ten hard-won quid, destined for the two-up school in a canvas tent behind the animal cages.

A pair of flashing fists delivered by a brown eyed youngster by name Dave Sands, knocked out Mick's two front teeth.

Sands was the boxing alias of the Ritchie family. David Sands Ritchie, and brothers Clement, Percy, George, Alfred and Russell, won more than 600 fights, nearly 250 by knockout. Wins included an Empire title, one Australasian crown, four Australian belts and three state championships.

Mick met Dave Sands in Burnt Ridge near Kempsey, and fought him in a warm-up stoush before the main contest which featured the elder Sands brother, who in his heyday, was touted as a successor to Les Darcy, but the bruising tent circuit eventually addled his brain.

After beating the bejesus out of Mick, Dave Sands won three major Australian divisions; middle, light heavy and heavyweight. Sands outclassed the favoured Dick Turpin in England for the Empire title, and threatened a thrashing for Randolph Turpin and Sugar Ray Robinson. A road smash robbed him of the chance of pulling on the gloves against both men. He died aged 26.

Later in life, Mick and legions of followers of the sweet science, reckoned Australia lost a gentlemen with Dave Sands' death, but as a puffy and bruised-faced youth in Burnt Ridge, a battered Mick Vaughan chucked in life on the land forever, and followed the country shows to Sydney.

"You wouldn't believe what I saw last night."

"What?" Frankie sensed fear in his mate's voice.

"The ambulance brought a derelict to Sydney Hospital Casualty. So much blood they couldn't find the wounds."

"What in Christ's name do you mean, Mick?"

"A bastard cut his dick off."

Frankie sprayed whiskey across the bar.

A passer-by found the bloodied body of Albert Greenfield sprawled beneath cardboard boxes near the Boy Charlton swimming pool. Mick, on duty as acting sergeant at Central Street, answered a panicky call from the Sydney Hospital Resident.

"Don't tell anybody, Frankie."

An ashen faced Frankie said, "No, I won't mate."

Similar attacks prompted fearful men to walk home two by two. Police vans patrolled the haunts of derelict men. Nervous landlords nailed shut boarding house windows, and locked and bolted doors after sunset. The boisterous, grimy streets of Sydney's eastern suburbs were abandoned to feral cats. The tabloids described the grisly crimes as the activity of the Mutilator Murderer.

"Are you going to Police Boys tomorrow morning? Walter's keen on three rounds."

"No" said Mick, "and I won't be there in the afternoon either. We've got to catch this bastard."

41

# Chapter Eight
# Hollywood George

Murray Dwyer, the gambling newsagent, walked into the bar, sat on a stool, flicked open the paper, adjusted spectacles, and removed a pencil from the top pocket of his shirt. "Schooner of Old, love," Murray said, nodding to Frankie and Mick.

"Not a word, Frankie."

"She's apples mate. Just get the fucking bastard. Better still, why don't you collar this mongrel?"

Frankie returns Murray's nod, winks goodbye to Mick, and pulls up a stool next to him.

"What do you fancy tomorrow?"

"Warrior."

"What's the tote?" Frankie lights a cigarette, and exhales smoke into Murray's face.

"Five to four on, and breathe your fucking smoke elsewhere."

"Sticking with the favourites, eh?" Frankie's tone is contemptuous.

"Then there's Sea Pigeon, at 13 to 2. One or the other's a cert. I might have a few bob," Murray smoothes the newspaper, and sips his beer.

"You'll never be a millionaire with just a few bob, Murray. Why don't you take a real punt? You've got the dough. George Edser put 500 to 800 on Chartwell in the Encourage Handicap last week. Went from 21 to 1, to 9 to 4, and George walked away with 50,000 quid."

Murray's eyes pop. "You are joking."

"No, I'm not. I thought you read the bloody newspapers. The stewards hauled him in for a 'please explain' following the race."

"Edser always gets away with it. He's connected. You gotta be in the know," Murray touches the side of his nose. "And you know bloody everything, Sugden," he says, turning the pages of the newspaper, and pretending to read.

"Tell you what, seeing you're such a hotshot, why don't I organise a big time bet just for you. What do you say? A fair dinkum, jumbo money wager. Have you got the guts for it, Hollywood Murray Dwyer?" Frankie laughs, and calls for more whiskey.

"How big?"

"You reckon Warrior tomorrow, right? There's a bloke staying upstairs carrying a wad thicker than your fist. A punter from Queensland."

"What's his moniker?"

"No names, no pack drill. He works on a cattle station outside Brisbane. What say I organise a private bet between you and this hick?"

"I'll think it over."

"You do that, me old China, because word around the traps is this Ringer bets on the proverbial two flies." Frankie gulps the whiskey.

The bar fills with familiar faces.

"Gotta get tea. Give me a shout." Frankie stumbles toward the bar door. Clouds scud low across the eastern sky. A fine mist dusts the pavement. Frankie mumbles a litany of preferred foods, and as the cold air ignites the liquor, he hears Walter's whistle in the distance.

Rain falls steadily. "Dead track tomorrow, like that poor mongrel with no prick."

He vomits into the gutter.

# Chapter Nine
# Credit Squeeze

The neon signs of King Street, Newtown, dim to a watery refraction in an unvarying downpour. Ian Flood, John's father, scurrying home in the night-time rush hour, endures a drenching from an arc of petrol-hued spray, thrown up by speeding cars veering close to the kerb. The constant rain quieted the otherwise boisterous Flood family, warm and dry in their terrace on Gallagher Street, Darlington, except for the youngest who fretted for his daddy. As Mavis scolded the child out of the kitchen, Ian sought shelter beneath the awning of H.G. Palmers, located near the intersection of Missenden Road.

Flickering shadows dance from a glowing black and white television set, on display in the store front window. A salesman sporting slicked-back Brylcreemed hair, motions Ian inside for a closer look.

"Give me a shout if I can help." The salesman's adenoidal voice sounds as unctuous as his dandruff-flecked coif. Ian, now mesmerised, watches the salesman switch the channel selector to the Youth Show, where Rolf Harris paints an interpretation of his hit song *Tie Me Kangaroo Down, Sport*. After adjusting the brightness, and with a knowing glance, he distorts the picture with a twiddle of the vertical hold.

"Needs an antenna for proper reception. We stock a large variety of easy-to-fit aerials. When it's installed on the roof, the little lady and the kiddies can watch television every day," he says with a practised Kolynos Smile.

Rolf Harris' slurping paint becomes the outline of a camel.

"How much?"

"You've chosen top of the range sir. For two hundred and nine pounds, eleven shillings, or twenty-three shillings a week on our exclusive hire purchase agreement, you have bagged the bargain of the week." The beaming salesman begins to count the pennies and pounds of a late Friday night bonus. "May I ask if you and the missus work?"

"I'm a toolmaker on the railways. There's plenty of overtime. The wife is a trained nurse at Royal Prince Alfred. We bought a Hillman Minx for nine hundred and seventy nine pounds a month ago."

"Go well?"

"Sure does. A ripper. Paid cash for it. Saved for nearly three years, but I'm afraid a television this good is beyond our means."

"Tell you what. I'll talk with the boss, and see if I can beat him down to twenty one shillings and sixpence a week. I'll come around to your house tomorrow, and help install the aerial."

The Three Stooges slap each other with comic sound-effect syncopation. Ian laughs. The clerk walks toward the rear of the shop, and vanishes behind a door marked Staff Only. Moments later the rotund store manager, hand out stretched, waddles toward his prey.

"Mister?"

"Ian Flood."

"Appropriate name for tonight." The manager's hand is soft and clammy.

"Come this way please. I have a standard contract waiting your signature. Bobby will drive you and the television home, and get it going with a set of rabbit ears."

"Terrific," Ian says as Moe Fine pokes Curly in the eye.

"Sign here, Mr Flood," and with a condescending flourish, the bespectacled manager proffers a gold fountain pen, but Ian hesitates. "The salesman said twenty one shillings and sixpence. This says twenty five shillings."

"The television is twenty one shillings and sixpence. The indoor and outside aerial come to an extra fifty pounds, making a total of two hundred and fifty pounds, or twenty five shillings a week. Hire purchase and a two-year back-to-store warranty is H.G. Palmer's specialty."

Moe slaps brother Larry Fine across the face.

"We're closing the store at six-thirty. It's a terrible night. Bobby's promised to install the telly. What more do you want Mr. Flood?"

Ian signed the agreement and, with interest, paid three hundred and seventy pounds for a much loved black and white twenty one-inch HMV Panoramic Console. Fuel and maintenance costs meant the Hillman ended up on blocks in the garage, as the Flood family struggled to keep up with the spiralling interest rates of the hire-purchased television.

...

"What clothes do you want pressed?"

"Jeans and a white tee shirt." John's response confirms Mavis' suspicion.

"Going out?"

"Tomorrow, if it stops raining."

"May I ask where?"

"Luna Park."

"Are you taking your brother?" but Mavis knows the answer before John speaks. "No, mum, I'm going on my own."

The front door opens with a clatter. Ian and Bobby the salesman, lug a heavy box into the family room.

"I bought a television. It's a beauty."

"How much did it cost, Ian?"

"We'll talk it over later. Give me a hand to get it unpacked. John. Go and get the extension lead from the garage, and fetch a pair of pliers while you're at it."

"May I borrow a towel please?" A drop of rainwater trickles the length of Bobby's red, pustulated nose.

The family assembled the television amid a cluster of packing debris, but despite placing the rabbit ears aerial in every corner of the lounge room, Bobby failed to tune-in a sharp image. John ran the lead up the stairs, and after an age of fine adjustments, a crisp picture flickered to monochrome life in time for the 8.00pm movie.

"Atmospheric interference, I suspect," Bobby maintains his tone of authority. "It'll be better when the external aerial is fixed to the roof. I'll help you install it tomorrow. Goodnight and happy viewing."

Ian walks Bobby to the front door, and then runs back to the parlour. Mavis, caught up in the excitement, brings sandwiches to the family room, and settles in for the first of many TV dinners.

As Eric Baume thundered out *Viewpoint* at 10.30pm, John went to bed, his jeans and tee shirt laying crumpled in the deserted dining room.

Rain spatters against the window pane. No matter how hard John tries, he cannot recall Dora's face, evoking instead the vague outline of a small, thin girl with sulky eyes. He falls asleep, whispering her name.

# Chapter Ten
# Mr Blue

Chirruping sparrows twitter a pale, watery morning. Downstairs, John warms the iron in chill silence, and smoothes wrinkles from his clothes.

Tufts of kapok, scattered beside the overturned cardboard box, litter the usually spotless parlour floor. Stacks of dirty plates sit forgotten on the lowboy. Shards of coloured wire coil amid abandoned shoes, crumpled blankets, and tea-leafed cups.

John's youngest brother sits cross-legged in front of the television, oblivious to the cold.

"What time did you get out of bed?"

"Six o'clock, but it showed a funny pattern with lines and crosses, and made a long humming sound, and switched off."

"The man is coming around this morning to help dad install the aerial. You can watch it for as long as you want."

"You going out?"

"Yep. Luna Park." John bites his lip, but the non-committal youngster says "See yah," and stares at Captain Fortune and Uncle Reg cavorting on a rickety wooden stage set, located in a tiny studio in semi-rural Willoughby.

"That was easy," but the crisp autumn air sends John back indoors for a khaki jacket. Finally, he closes the front door with a soft emphatic click. Freedom. Walter Sugden, walking in the opposite direction, whistles a greeting.

"Going to Police Boys, Bug?"

"Yeah. You look sharp. Where are you travelling?"

"Out for a while. You know."

"Sure Flood, pull the other one. Who is she?" Walter unslings his duffel bag and drops it to the wet pavement.

"There's no girl, Bug. I got to go."

"See you later and remember training."

The tram takes an age to arrive. John fidgets for the six-penny fare to the Bennelong Point end of Circular Quay.

The Customs House clock chimes for 8.30pm.

What to do for an hour and a half? Walk to the Rocks? Will she come? She'll forget. She won't turn up; why should she? But he recalls Dora's adamant voice, ten o'clock, Circular Quay. But where? The Quay is huge. People everywhere. Which end?

"The Luna Park ferry," he says aloud. A startled passer-by responds, "Pardon me?" John, abashed, replies, "Nothing. Sorry."

The Customs House Clock ticks to twenty-five minutes to nine.

Street sweepers push hard-bristled brooms along the gutters. Barrow men unpack fruit and vegetables for the Saturday morning trade. A yawning barman, cigarette in hand, hoses the footpath in front of a pub. Pigeons drink from pools of rain water, as squalling seagulls shriek and scrabble over a scrap of soggy potato chip. Steam-powered ferries churn white water to a dead stop, touching creaking wharf beams. A procession of electric trains clatters overhead and the hands of the Customs House Clock mark twenty minutes to nine.

Éamon Casey, walking to the Opera House building site, greets John standing in front of a quayside milk bar.

"Kenny said the pre-season training went well at North Sydney."

"Sure did, Mr. Casey. I think we've got a real chance this year." John shifts from foot to foot.

"Mum and dad well, I hope?"

"Yes, they're good, thanks. Dad bought a TV last night."

"I prefer the radio meself. Things are changing fast these days. You've put on a spurt, young John."

"Suppose so."

"Have a good day. I'm off to work for the capitalists."

"The who?"

"The big people who want to bugger the little people. Do you see those houses high on the hill?" Éamon points toward Millers Point. "I guarantee the bastards will try to demolish them, and send the poor families to god-knows-where. Two big companies plan to develop the land around the wharves, and turn the place into another Potts Point. Turf everyone out on their ear, but we'll stop 'em, don't you worry. Regards to your family, John."

"Say good day to Ken for me, Mr. Casey." The Customs House clock ticks a quarter to nine.

Across the city in Darlington, the Ringer from Queensland reaches for a packet of Senior Service cigarettes, lights up, coaxes a deep drag from the glowing tip, and switches on the radio. Then with one hand behind his head, he lies back on the pillow, and listens to the public house come to life. The monotone nasal voices of radio tipsters drone selections for the day's race meeting. He shaves in front of a small mirror, savouring the aroma of sizzling bacon and frying eggs wafting the length of the corridor, and seeping beneath his door.

Dark blue trousers offset a white shirt, and matching white socks. A neat Windsor knot complements a pale blue tie, and shiny black, pointed-toe shoes. A splash of bay rum tingles razor-smoothed cheeks. A squirt of Spruso darkens a mop of tight curly red hair. Then, with cigarettes in hand, and a thick plug of pound notes deep in pocket, the Ringer slips on a matching blue suit coat, and double skips each stair tread to the dining room.

In the newsagency Murray supervises a rapid trade in Saturday newspapers. Mick, yawning at the end of a police night shift, sips a cup of tea, and as Walter pounds upper cuts into the heavy bag, the Customs House Clock reaches ten to nine.

The Ringer scans the sports pages; Tony Madigan up against Ken Marshall at the Sydney Stadium; then, on a news page, the story of two young men attempting to evict the manager of the Anglican Press in Queen Street, Chippendale.

During the fracas a man identified as Kerry copped a black eye.

He smiles at the antics of *Boofhead* and *Ace O'Hara,* and marks an X against *Swedish Love Idyll* screening at the Gala cinema. "Have a dekko tonight, if things go well. Blow a few quid at the Latin Quarter. Maybe meet a sheila."

Day-old newspapers provide crucial tote variations, and mid-week tips for the upcoming races. He whistles softly at the Opera House Lottery winners' list; first prize 100,000 pounds won by *Self* syndicate of Edward Street, Bondi. "Lucky bastard," he says, and eats a large country breakfast. He drinks two pots of strong black tea, smokes several cigarettes, and circles Foolish Empire on the form guide.

Outside the pub Lonnie Donegan warbles *My Old Man's a Dustman.* Two dogs snarl and fight on the street. A bottle-o loads clattering wooden boxes onto a horse-drawn cart. The nag, wary of the snarling dogs, whinnies and stamps its front hoof, and deposits a pile of steaming dung that smells of hay and the race track.

Frankie Sugden strolls past the bottle-o into the backyard, and nods to the publican.

"He's in the dining room."

# Chapter Eleven
# Mirror Maze

Ten o'clock. Frazzled parents and excited children nudge each other across the gangplank aboard the ferry to Milsons Point. At the last moment John jumps the widening gap between wharf and boat, and squeezes through the crowd to the stern where he thought he had glimpsed Dora. He cannot find her in the crush.

A deckhand flicks the mooring rope off the bollard, closes and locks the safety rail as the creaking wooden scow backs away from its mooring, turns bow-on and chugs across the harbour. Small boats skim the breeze, their wind-filled sails slap against straining steel spars. As the grey, shadowy underbelly of the Harbour Bridge darkens the sparkling water, John recalls Tony's words during their long walk across the bridge deck earlier in the week: "Bloody long way to fall."

Silver sunlight shafts flash and glitter off the rotating arms of the Ferris Wheel as muffled screams of delight whiplash from the Big Dipper.

The deckhand, resplendent in gloves and sunglasses, lassoes a rusty post, and as the taut rope strains and engines roar into reverse, awestruck children gawp at the grimacing Luna Park face.

John, first off, sits on a grassy verge, and as the ferry chugs across Lavender Bay toward McMahon's Point, a light tap tickles his right shoulder.

"Hello John," Dora says smiling, and skips toward the leering face.

"Are you some kind of sprite?" John calls behind her.

"That's for you to discover," she says. Tiny, faded blue flowers decorate a simple white dress. A shock of bobbed auburn hair shimmers in the morning light.

"I bought you a ferry ticket," John says with delighted exasperation.

"Thank you. I'll use it on the way home." They stand next to each other in a queue. Dora watches John's eyes dip and scan the orb of her breast. As she catches his glance, she looks toward a trio of boys, turns back and smiles.

"Meet you in front of the Penny Arcade," but before John can say "where", Dora vanishes into the throng.

A gaggle of girls mingling outside the dark, cavernous arcade clutch tiny handbags. Dora is not among them. The swivelling eyes of the open-mouthed Laughing Clowns follow John's impatient pacing by the Ferris Wheel, as streams of giggling couples and families, climb into and out of the clanging, suspended cabins.

John counts forty-three horses, a lion, a griffin and two chariots on the Merry-Go-Round. He saunters toward the musty old Palais de Dance, a converted vehicular ferry that plied the harbour in the days and years before the great grey span of the bridge joined Sydney north to south. Time ticks noiselessly amid the dark shadows of the dance palace. Arthur Barton's haggard wall murals keep watch on ardent, silent lovers seeking privacy for a first kiss.

For the price of a penny, a fortune-telling booth named, Try Another About Love, cranks out a small voucher. John places the green ticket inside a pocket in his khaki jacket.

Intersecting lines cross and criss-cross a black handprint. Each line points to signs of the zodiac decorating the rusted exterior of Mastermind; The Hand of Knowledge. Within sits an old, mysterious male dummy, inscrutable in the dim-lit cubicle, and locked away for eternity.

Boys in leather jackets flipper pin-ball machines and smoke cigarettes. A young girl feeds tokens into a glass cage, and guides a clumsy mechanical claw toward a coveted pink kewpie doll, or a skeleton-shaped ash tray.

The sun shines bright and warm outside Penny Arcade; the autumnal air aromatic with sweet toffee apples and sticky fairy floss.

*Cathy's Clown* blares near the Rotor; the lyric distorted by spinning screams spiralling from the vortex. The Big Boys stand high and bright above Coney Island.

Bobby Rydell's *Swinging School* taunts all to walk the Turkey Trot, and pass through rubber prison bars. Groups of boys hang back to watch an updraft of warm air disturb those crossing the scissoring planks. Canny girls clutch skirts close to their thighs, and safely cross the wind vent. Then with squealing virtue intact, they turn and poke out defiant tongues.

Dora stoops beneath an entrance to a set of steep wooden stairs rising to the Devils Drop, but disappears when John's turn comes to complete the dizzying slide. He sees her atop the crest of the Joy Wheel, which spins ever faster and forces the strongest from its burnished wooden dome.

Dora is not among the laughing, tumbling throng, skidding onto the cushion-strewn floor.

John's image leers from a row of distorting mirrors; pointed head, tiny legs, now fat, now thin. Dora's reflection appears in a long mirror. John spins on his heel and curses. A sequence of revolving mirrors reflects a tilted floor inside Davy Jones Locker. Gurgling water bubbles in aquariums, creating the effect of a sunken ship, with angled prow jutting from the seafloor.

A painted mural of a bow-legged sailor beckons all to crouch and enter. John wriggles between the legs into the Mirror Maze, and sees a myriad of images stare from every angle. As the path narrows, he comes to a dead-end and studies his agitated, glowering face in a mirror.

A girl giggles. "I'm here John." Dora's laugh echoes throughout the maze.

"Where are you?" but John sees multiples of himself.

"Here." Dora's replicate coaxes him forward, and as he walks toward her image, he bumps into a large, polished lens.

"Stop playing around." A gathering of spectres mimic every movement as cheval glass corridors decorated with sparkling beads, coil into the distant, brilliant labyrinth.

"I've got you now, I can see you." But Dora laughs and the imprint of her back slips away.

"Come and find me, John."

"Stay where you are. Don't move." Again John stands at the maze entranceway as streams of laughing people creep beneath the sailors' legs. He runs once more along the original path, but turns right into a circular chamber illuminated by a burnished ceiling. "Dora," he calls, but a chorus of voices echo, "Dora, Dora" as dozens of unfamiliar faces walk forward and away. "I'm here." As he turns, his reflection stands next to her image which skips away to the accompaniment of a laughing repetition of "I'm here."

John follows a bewildered file of boys and girls, smells fresh, briny air, and stumbles into the sunlight. Dora falls to her knees, clutching her sides with laughter.

"I'm hungry." Dora says and scoots toward a crowded milk bar.

In the River Caves John placed an arm around Dora's shoulder, bent his face to her hair, smelt fragrant shampoo, and kissed her lightly on the neck. Arm in arm they watched Toyland become the Wild Wood of the Canadian Rockies, before Scott in the Antarctic, and marvelled at King

Neptune atop a giant crab. Dora, balancing a tiny lacquered Chinese chest on her lap, looked unblinking at John.

Dr Pandora Hope and John Flood raised four children in a restored terrace house in Dargan Street, Glebe. Dora now lectures part-time at Sydney University. John manages a small art gallery on St John's Road. Deep in their attic, a tattered green card nestles in the innermost chamber of a brittle, papier-mâché puzzle chest. The fading words on the card read, *love sought is good, but given unsought is better.*

# Chapter Twelve
# Theme to a Summer Place

"Mind if I join you?" Frankie Sugden draws up a stool.

"Suit yourself."

"Enjoying your stay in Sydney?"

"No complaints. What can I do for you?"

"Fancy a heart starter. Whiskey?"

"No thanks."

Frankie removes a cigarette from the pack, and taps twice at the loose tobacco shreds escaping from the white paper tube.

"I might be inclined to do a little something for you."

"Since when did bookies do punters favours?"

"Fair point, but seeing as you're a betting man, I thought you might be interested in a bigger punt."

"I might. What's in it for you?"

"Leery bastard, aren't you."

The Ringer taps a Senior Service cigarette on the table, lights up, flicks the smouldering match onto the floor and asks again, "What's in it for you?"

"Five per cent off the top." Frankie follows the Ringer's eyes chart the rise of the curling smoke.

"What are you thinking Frankie?

"Mate, that's for me to know, so don't fret."

"What sort of money?"

"Good enough for a boy from the bush."

"Who's the mark?"

"Murray Dwyer. A local businessman." Frankie mutters under his breath, "and a fucking coppers' nark."

"What did you say?

"Never you mind what I said."

"Not a fan, eh."

"Fan! I hate his fucking guts."

"So which race are we talking about?"

"The fifth."

"What's he on?"

"Sea Pigeon or Warrior." The Ringer exhales smoke, and with pen balanced between first and second fingers, taps on his selection in barrier position four, the fifth race. Odds quoted 100 to 1.

"See you later this afternoon, Mr. Sugden."

"At five per cent, you can count on it." Frankie walks to the ladies' parlour.

The Ringer orders lemonade, lime and bitters. "Hard stuff, eh, pal?" The barman glances at the redheaded man.

"Need to keep a clear head, mate, so give me a nod when Murray comes in." He glides a ten pound note onto the bar and motions the barman to keep the change, but as the bar tender picks up the tenner, the Ringer leans across the counter and whispers, "Next time, mind your own fucking business." The waiter's face turns white, and with change in hand, walks to the far end of the saloon.

The droning radio spits and crackles. Regular drinkers perched on favourite stools, hunch over lucky tables, flicking ash from burning cigarettes into reeking ashtrays. A weather-beaten cocky outside the pub, watching for coppers, dozes in the sun. Frankie sits beside a bank of four telephones in a dark corner, nodding at each man who places a bet.

The loose limbed Ringer sits cool and calm; his wad thicker at Frankie's expense.

"That bloody kid takes hours to finish the friggin' paper run. I'm damned if I know what he gets up to. Schooner of Old and a nip of Dewar's," Murray raps at the bar.

"You skinny prick," Frankie mutters under his breath.

Totes for race four list Sea Pigeon at 13 to 2 and favourite, Warrior at 5 to 4, with Foolish Empire sitting way out on a rotten limb at 100 to 1. The Ringer leans back in his chair. A .25 pistol presses the small of his back.

Murray drains the whiskey, and gulps his beer. Frankie moves to the main bar. The publican calls to the barman. The cocky saunters inside the saloon, dazzled by the transition from light to dark.

"Murray, me old China. Meet a mate of mine. Mr Blue, this is the man we've been discussing."

"And with this sharp-looking suit, your nickname's got to be Bluey."

"Only fools call me that name."

"Is this a joke, Frankie?"

The Ringer places a wad of cash on the table, and with a jerk of his chin says, "No joke, Murray."

Frankie signals both men to the ladies' parlour. As the trio move away from the bar, the cocky, watching the parley unfold, crosses the street, enters a red pill box telephone booth, and dials a number. The radio plays *A Theme to a Summer Place*.

"Let me put you straight. You mention my kid again and I'll rip your ugly fucking head off your shoulders, and kick your soggy brains into next week."

Beads of sweat glisten on Murray's forehead.

"Race four starts in ten minutes. Pick your mount, and call your bet on the starting price nominated by my connection. Loser has twenty-four hours to pay the winner. My commission is five per cent. Debt settled here tomorrow at noon. Minimum bet five hundred quid, with money up front, and proof of cover on the bet, or else."

"Or else what?"

"Don't look for Mick Vaughan, Murray. He won't be back here for weeks. He's after a bloke who's slashing off coves' cocks, so nominate your cover, or show the dough. No cover, no bet."

The Ringer picks up a bundle of notes. "Count it, Frankie. There's at least ten thousand pounds. Most of it was yours."

Murray pulls out a neat billfold, and peels off five hundred pounds.

"The deeds to the shop are in the safe. Bona fide."

Frankie thrusts a thumb into the air. "Kosher."
"Better be."

"It is, it is." Murray says, but the Ringer places the pistol on the table and says, "It fucking better be, cunt."

"Put that away, for Christ's sake."

"What the fuck is this, Sugden," but the radio announcer's drone of the totes interrupts Murray's frantic rant.

Unblinking the Ringer says, "Five hundred quid Foolish Empire."

"Five hundred on Sea Pigeon. There is no way in this fucking world this nag can get up at a hundred to one," Murray says. Frankie glances from one man to the other. "Do I have a bet?" Murray and the Ringer pass their five hundred pounds to Frankie.

"No way it can win."

Frankie picks up a red telephone, dials and repeats the words; "Sea Pigeon a firm seven and a half to one, yep, and Foolish Empire out at 110 to one." Then with arched eyebrows Frankie says, "Are we done?" Murray, staring at the dirty wad of money next to the pistol, nods in unison with the Ringer.

"Done."

# Chapter Thirteen
# Eternity

Murray gulps damp, smoky air as the chilled plume of exhaled breath billows skyward toward a dim lamp light.  The words 'Foolish Empire', beat a tattoo across his temple veins.

Bea Miles, slumped in a darkened doorway, mutters snatches from *The Dark Lady*. A reeking she-cat stretches and rolls in the gutter. A screeching tom mounts, and bites into her neck.

A wizened man wearing a grey Macintosh, a battered homburg on the back of his head, sits frozen on his haunches, but for the articulation of his arm.

A distant ship horn announces the flow of tide. Seamen call to one another in voices from other worlds, and in a dark, distant street, a pair of slow moving stiletto heels echo across cobblestones.

"I'll get those fucking bastards one by one, and their mates, and I'll kill their fucking families." Murray stumbles headlong across the slippery pavement, and paws shoe leather across an indelible yellow chalk mark, attempting to erase the first letter of the word Eternity.

# Chapter Fourteen
## Lolly Legs

If the price of admission to a Saturday game fell beyond scarce funds, you stayed at home listening to Frank Hyde's call on the Stromberg Carlson radio, punching the air at a try, or hissing a missed goal. Those with money saved from a paper round or a milk run, fought their way to the dressing shed entrance, waiting for their side to run onto the field. Each favoured player earned bursts of applause. Autograph hunters colonised the tunnel for the final whistle, clapping a victory or consoling a loss, but their mission always remained obtaining the magic signature. A scrawled dedication, more mud than ink, guaranteed the owner's status at school the following week. Prized autographs adorned double-sided bubble gum cards. Envious mates coughed up a zac a look, or attempted to parley a valuable card in marble alley. A proud owner might weigh up a swap or sale, as part of a set. Value fluctuated with a win or a loss, or the skill of an individual player; all the more reason to cheer a try, or call "lolly legs" before an opponent's goal kick. Swap cards, autographs, and battered-faced men spruiking hot doggies, comprised football's winter mosaic.

The under fourteens caught footie fever; each team member fancied their face emblazoned on a coloured bubble gum card. Walter imagined catching an impossible pass. Enzo dreamt of floating inches above the ground in a flying tackle.

The season passed as if a mirror of the first grade comp. The Bankstown school players proved as tough as their first grade heroes, and Balmain kids played a fast, flashy game with high drop punts a speciality. The Saints forward pack, rucked hard up the middle, but the Darlington fourteens modelled their game on the swift, mobile Rabbitohs.

Coach and supporters expected everyone to attend weekend derbies, but cousins Bill and Declan demurred, choosing to spend Saturdays at Redfern Oval, copying their heroes.

During a school game, recalling the deeds of a favoured champion, one or both cousins flashed down the wing. Declan ran for a well-aimed drop kick from the fullback, or Billy followed-up a bruising back line movement. If either cousin failed to score a try, they compensated by gaining precious positional yards, thus granting a breather to the heavy, grinding forwards.

While Terry and Quentin served as school clowns, Declan ruled as the undisputed football prankster. In one memorable tussle with North Sydney Boys High, Declan scooped up the ball, turned and ran toward his own touch line. Chaos erupted. Walter bellowed, and Uncle Jimmy on the side-line near burst a blood vessel.

The opposing players stopped and watched. A big mistake. Declan ran full bore toward his own line with the ball tucked under his left arm. Inches before colliding with the post, Declan crooked his right arm around the upright, allowing speed to slingshot him from the post, and off to his opponents' unguarded goal line. Declan scored the match winner. The North Sydney players screamed in protest but the referee judged it a fair try.

Billy's favourite trick at the end of training was to sit on his haunches holding the ball, before leap-frogging to a sprint, followed by a bolt for the sheds; one hundred yards in twelve seconds. Other players followed listlessly. Meanwhile Billy, stretched out on a bench, tossed the ball lazily into the air saying, "What kept youse?"

Both cousins sparkled on field, but off the paddock remained aloof and reticent.

At the conclusion of a well-played away match, the losing captain invited the victors into the clubhouse for lemonade. The cousins invariably declined, after a glance by an official signalled their racial status. Jimmy, Bill and Declan gnawed stalks of grass to quench their thirst.

Attitudes were different at Redfern Oval. Each weekend the cousins barracked and skylarked, roaring for either the All Blacks or La Perouse United.

Billy studied the skill of individual players as a punter follows the form guide. He stuck a double page photograph of an up-and-coming fifteen-year-old named Eric Simms onto his bedroom wall, and talked to the picture every night.

Several times during the year, South Sydney scouts sat in the stand with Jimmy Bomer and Graeme Davidson, a rabid Rabbitohs' fan who ignored the social code, and became a devotee, and eventually an official, of Aboriginal divisional matches.

Corowa, Saddler, Simms, Williamson; a parade of talent passed through the Redfern turnstiles, mesmerising the crowd, but a young

Arthur Beetson, the greatest forward in the world, towered over them all. Generations of kids and adults screamed themselves hoarse over Big Artie's exploits.

At the tail end of the season, Jimmy escorted two country men around the Redfern Oval environs. Both men wore wide-brimmed, sweat stained cowboy hats, and long, grey-flecked beards. They teased tobacco between their palms, and rolled cigarettes single-handed, but politely declined proffered bottles of beer. They had come to Redfern Oval to watch the games. Jimmy pointed out a particular player during a dazzling passage, and spoke full speed with the country duo.

The bearded men unsettled Declan, but curiosity bettered him late one Saturday afternoon. Observing from a distance, Declan eventually snuck up behind the men, trying to eavesdrop on their conversation, but he did not comprehend their language.

"They come from Walgett," Jimmy said. "Your country. One or two of you young fellows might go up and play a few games with the Warriors, eh?"

"Why would I want to go to bloody Walgett?" Declan's reply, and impudent stare, demanded a riposte. Jimmy paused before answering.

"Because it is where you was born. You came to Redfern as a baby. Auntie Maudie and I took you in, and raised you as our son." Jimmy looped an arm around his nephew.

"Your mother Marie, Maude's sister, was sixteen when you was born. The local pastor notified the district Protector, who recommended you for adoption in Cootamundra, but to save you, Marie, your mother," Jimmy paused, "sent you 'ere to Redfern. Now it's time for you to go to your Country. You're nearly a man, Declan. Fourteen's the age you supposed to learn our law."

Jimmy pointed toward the two country men, one of whom fixed Declan with an unblinking gaze.

"He's your father.

"It's different for us. We got our own laws; our way of doing things.

"Older men marry young women; nothing wrong with that; and children reared by their relatives, but what is wrong is taking a child from his mother and adopting out their aboriginality.

"When your kin visit, you are responsible for them. Same goes when they visit you.

"In Sydney, our law has nearly disappeared, but that doesn't mean *we've* gone though. Most gubbas probably never seen a black fulla. They think we were wiped out, but we still 'ere, livin' on our land."

"This country," Jimmy waves an embracing arm across Redfern Oval, "called Eora. Out Emu Plains they called Dharruk, and in North Sydney, Cammeraygal.

"Remember when we trained there at the beginning of the season and I introduced you and Billy to George Ambrum? He knows everyone. Aboriginal people live on all the shores of this 'arbour.

"When I was a kid, me and a cobber caught the Manly ferry. We'd earn a few bob at the wharf, and then walk back 'ome. Take us a week. We'd go around Dobroyd, then toward Seaforth. My mate had a tinny stashed in the bush. We'd paddle over to a place called Sugar Loaf Bay, collect pipis and oysters at low tide, fish for flathead and yellowtail, then walk up the creek into the mangroves, and cook up the lot on an old fireplace for a feed.

"Aboriginal camp sites all across Sydney. Paintings over in Leichhardt, and up in Cromer, and Elanora Heights. Big kangaroo carved in a rock at Guringai, but most people 'ave forgotten the law." Jimmy swigs a bottle of cola. "Not in Walgett, though. Law still strong."

Declan glanced toward the bearded man, now grinning through a gap in his teeth. Jimmy points to the LaPer team scoring a blistering try. "That mob goes all the way to Nowra, Cudmirrah, and all that country." A stray dog wanders toward Jimmy. He pats it behind the ears.

Jimmy takes a battered cardboard folder out of his shirt pocket, flicks it open and shows Declan the contents.

"This 'ere an Exemption Certificate, but we call it a dog tag. I still got to carry it everywhere I go in Australia.

"This is gubba law.

"You'll get one. At the moment you're too young for pubs, or travel, but you'll want to do those things, like any other person, and the time's getting close. You carry your dog tag, or else."

"Or else what?"

"Go to jail. We can't even play sport without one. This bloody thing means you're a professional. You're not eligible for amateur sports.

"'Ave you wondered why Aboriginal people play this code?" Jimmy points at the United/All Blacks game thundering on the oval.

"Cheaper than cricket mate, no pads or white trousers. League's professional, but Rugby Union is amateur, and that means no blacks." Jimmy snaps the folder shut. The crowd cheers another try. The dog catches a new scent, and wanders away.

"I'm not saying you should go up bush; your home's 'ere. You can stay as long as you want, but it might do you good; get some fresh air during the next school holidays, eh? Think it over," Jimmy says, and sucks a stalk of grass.

Declan felt a stone fall on his heart. His so-called father, a smiling, coal-black man with a visage resembling photographs he had seen in *Pix* magazine, seems as unreal as Jimmy's assertions.

"These things don't happen in Australia," Declan says. "They don't take babies from their mothers," but Jimmy's cardboard dog tag served as proof.

The football match ends, and as the afternoon light fades, crowds of laughing people drift toward bus and tram stops.

"I'll introduce you."

Shivering in the evening chill, Declan shoves both hands deep into his jacket pockets, and feels a square of cardboard beneath his handkerchief.

"All right."

Declan removes the football bubble gum card from his pocket, stares at the picture, tears the image to shreds, and throws the pieces into a garbage bin.

# Chapter Fifteen
# Laurel and Hardy

Sydney University bewitched Anthony (Tony) Moroney, who with jet black hair and model looks, passed hot summer days swimming in the blue, chlorine water of nearby Victoria Park pool. In the winter months, Tony kicked a football around the enclosed Sydney University ovals.

Brothers Harlan and Eugene considered Tony a candidate for a scholarship, based on excellence in all subjects, and the added prowess of an all-round athlete.

In the rarefied world of the bursary, a lowered eye might mean acceptance, but an unblinking stare, a letter of rejection. Tony managed the many bursary obstacles with aplomb.

Quentin Gallagher idolised Tony, who like the entire team, ignored his stunted right leg, the legacy of a mild bout of infant polio. The withered limb did not impede Quentin's schoolboy football career, and he was a half back without peer in the junior competitions.

Ruddy-faced scouts from Newtown and South Sydney, who monitored schoolboy games, marked him as a potential recruit. In his fourteenth year, the shortened leg did not appear noticeable, nor was it an impairment to on-field speed or skill, but as Quentin grew the final few inches to full height, the affliction became apparent, and with it smouldered the temper of a small man.

Schoolmates dubbed Tony and Quentin, Laurel and Hardy. Quentin used the solemn Tony as a comic foil in an endless round of pranks and pratfalls. During one game, Quentin sprinkled itching powder inside Tony's jersey, before scurrying around the field, darting away from the infuriated Tony who ran, stopped, scratched, cursed and ran once more.

"Poor old Tony," said Quentin. "Not a hair out of place." Both renewed the sprint and chase, amid a chain of curses and scoffing laughter.

# Chapter Sixteen
## Bat wing

Frankie Sugden devised a plan for a surreptitious coming-of-age evening by persuading Walter, Quentin and Tony to deliver a bolt of Christmas cloth to a distant aunt living in a dilapidated boarding house atop William Street Kings Cross.

After tea and small talk with the aunt, the trio could take a quick look around the Cross, before returning home. Frankie knew Walter would refuse the chore without money, so a fiver became the primary inducement. When split three ways, and with Quentin and Tony's dosh, the threesome seemed primed for a night to remember.

Kings Cross straddles eastern and central Sydney. The loping promontory of Potts Point, and the curved inlet of Elizabeth Bay, lured wealthy merchants who, from the time of the Rum Corps, bartered the commerce of a prosperous colony growing along the shores of the most well-favoured port in the world.

By the end of the Victorian era, the wide boulevard of William Street hosted an array of boarding houses, which catered for country travellers of both genders. These cheap and cheerful digs enticed generations of the young of New South Wales to sample city life beyond the clutches of an insufferable rural patriarchy.

Razor gangs and hardworking prostitutes lived cheek by jowl with the Kings Cross gentry. Each night, slatterns and sailors sought single rooms in one of the numerous bed and breakfast hotels, hell-bent on a raucous bout of revelry.

In the years after World War One, beret-wearing artists, sipping coffee and quaffing aperitifs, applied for art classes. Discreet announcements for 'still life with nude', guaranteed an eager line of youths, recently returned from the killing fields of Ypres and Fromelles.

Aspiring writers recited the poetry of Stéphane Mallarmé to girls with rosebud lips, or chased the acrid opium dragon in dingy dens in Dixon Street, Chinatown.

Baccarat, Fan Tan and the roulette wheel mesmerised the luckless and the lucky, who gambled away their lives in gentlemen's clubs on Darlinghurst Road. Night after night, inveterate sybarites, jaundiced by the ecstasy of flesh, recounted lurid tales to legions of the immature, who sought out pleasure domes hidden behind locked doors in Kings Cross laneways and streets. For the price of a few pounds, a young man or woman could enjoy a night of fable in Sydney's underworld.

Murray Dwyer haunted these Kings Cross flesh pits and bars. After being skinned by the Ringer and Frankie Sugden, the bankrupt newsagent carried a cosh in his jacket pocket for protection. Murray lived off the earnings of poor, pocked-face molls and gambled their income at Thommo's Two-up School. Late at night, prostrate on a filthy bed in a shabby dosshouse, Murray dreamt of vengeance. This evening, fate delivered the means of retribution in the guise of three wide-eyed boys.

Frankie's aunt warned the trio to catch a tram back to Darlington after sunset. Fat chance. With cash in pocket, Tony, Quentin and Walter chose to walk; not westward to the mills and cobblestones of Darlington, but east toward the glittering lights of Kings Cross.

Garish neons flashed advertisements for cigarettes and hotels, along streets crowded with sailors on leave from warships moored at Garden Island. Old men picked at garbage bins, while smart young couples disappeared into lofty apartments. Spruikers bawled their wares, as confident office workers weaved through the irrational crowd. Well-coiffed fashionable women glanced nonchalantly at the throng from the comfort of green, padded leather booths in gilt, plush restaurants.

Tony scanned the unfamiliar faces, while the irrepressible Quentin bobbed and weaved in and out of the gathering. Walter rubbed sweaty palms against his jeans.

"Let's get a drink."

"Sure. My throat's as dry as a Pommies' towel."

From the street, the tiny, dark cafe appeared devoid of patrons, but inside a slow jazz bass riff reverberated from a record player. Roasting coffee and pungent cigarette smoke scented the room. The owner, a slight, waspish man with an unusual accent, darted behind the bar, glowering at the threesome.

"What you want in here, eh? You got money? Show me. Otherwise get out. You understand?" he said, dark brown eyes glittering with malice.

A voluptuous woman's voice whispered from the dimmest corner of the bistro. "Let them be, Yanni. They are so charming."

"We've got cash, mate. I want a cup of tea and a toasted ham sandwich."

"I don't sell tea."

"Fine. Make it coffee then," said Quentin. The others nodded despite having never tasted the beverage.

Tony called for a soft drink. Quentin placed a ten shilling note on the table. Yanni snapped up the bill, and flounced behind the bar. The jazz droned as Turkish tobacco smoke curled across the room. Yanni returned with coffee and sandwiches on a tray, and placed the change on the table with an indifferent glance.

The unseen woman approached.

"Shall I read your palm and tell your fortune? I have a crystal ball." Her voice is deep and ardent. Plucked eyebrows arch upward in a wispy, delicate line across her forehead and a slash of scarlet lipstick across her thin, sharp lips accentuates pallid flesh. Long manicured nails stretch from the tips of elongated fingers and a loose, shabby cloak drapes across her shoulders. The trio is mesmerised.

"No, Rosie. Not now. It is too early. Please, put the bloody crystal ball away, will you, for Christ's sake!" Yanni whines, as if a spitting cat, but Rosie hisses back, "Coffee, darling. Pronto." The tension dissipates. The bistro door opens to the chime of a bell, and a wiry man with wispy hair snaking from beneath a dark beret, moves toward the bar.

"Gavin, darling. Look what I've found. A glorious trinity of boys. Aren't they sweet?" Gavin grasps Rosie's proffered hand and kisses her palm.

"You have brought me youth. I am in your eternal debt, but first, I must eat. Macchiato, Yanni. Bread and mortadella, and black olives if you please. I will not live a minute longer without coffee." Holding Rosie by the elbow, the pair glides to a dusky corner of the café, and evaporates behind a curtain of pungent, blue smoke.

"Let's go," says Walter. Tony, last to leave, turns and peers toward the couple. Two glinting green eyes return his gaze. "We look forward to the pleasure of your pleasure."

"Jeez, who are they? What a bloody weird lot! Did you see her face?" As the exclamations and questions tumble one over the other, Tony declares time for home. Walter and Quentin agree, but Kings Cross chooses not to release them from its maw.

Gangs of youths creep along Darlinghurst Road, gawking at strip tease parlours, urging one another inside. Buskers play gum leaves or violins. Christians preach the evils of drink and debauchery. Pimps curse and pull at prostitutes tallying their wares for drunken sailors. A saxophone wails in the distance. Kerb-coasting cars honk, as touts stop unwary couples, luring them toward dim doorways. Separated by the throng, the boys push through the crowd. Quentin laughs at stern-faced Tony. Walter, chest puffed out, struts ahead of the others, stopping to watch a man play musical notes on a band saw adorned with a dozen tame budgerigars. A fight erupts. A Polynesian woman, wreathed in waist length hair, kicks and punches a bald-headed man who falls to his knees, as much from humility as the severity of the beating. A rabble circles the ruckus, goading the woman on. A Black Maria pulls over. The crowd melts away as the police hustle the brawlers into the back of the van.

Murray watches the boys watching the street fight, and choosing his moment, grabs Walter by the shoulder and drags him into an open doorway. Tony and Quentin follow. Quentin ducks under a bouncer's legs. Tony's size parleys him past a pug on the door. A low hubbub of voices saturates the large room. Tony strains in the darkness for Walter. "He's gotta be in here somewhere."

"What do you kids want?" A barrel-chested ruddy-faced man grabs both by the scruff of the neck, but Quentin manages to twist out of the grasp, turns his face to the man and says, "We want a beer, right? We come in for a lousy drink, and you blokes put the hard hand on us."

"You're too bloody young for beer, get out." The man reaches, but Quentin squirms away.

"I'm a jockey right! Don't let me size fool yah, pal."

"You're not a jockey, Quentin," says Tony.

"Yeah, well, I'm an apprentice. We're meeting a mate of ours, name of Sugden." Recognition of the name softens barrel chest's expression, and he loosens his grip on Tony.

"Who else," he demands.

"Mick Vaughan. Jimmy Bomer."

"All right, have your beer, but I've got my eye on you two. Make trouble and bang." The big man punches his fist. At the bar he says "A middy for the tall one, and give short arse here a Depth Charge, and see he drinks it. On the house."

"Who's he?" Quentin asks the barman.

"Don't ask. If you survive this turn, mate, he might let you stick around."

Quentin grabs the whiskey, swallows it in a gulp, and drains the icy beer.

"You're supposed to take a swig out of the middy, drop the whiskey glass into the beer then sip it, stupid." The barman mops the bar and moves away.

"I gotta sit down."

"What do you mean, a bloody apprentice jockey, Gallagher? You are such a bullshit artist," but Quentin does not hear the words. His lips whiten. His face turns grey.

"Toilet." The barman and red-faced manager laugh, as Quentin retches his heart out in the lavatory.

Walter watches his pals' shenanigans from a shadowy corner booth at the back of the cocktail lounge. Murray sits on his right, a man with a deep red welt across his cheek, on his left.

"Seems as though short arse can toss it back."

"Or toss it up," Murray says, as Tony guides the still retching Quentin from the toilet.

"Did your old man put you up to this, or did you just wander up here by yourselves?"

"I dropped off a delivery at an aunt's place, and we decided to spend dad's five pounds."

"My money, I'll wager."

"Look, Mr Dwyer, I want to go home, so if you don't mind."

"Stick around for a while, sonny. Have a couple of laughs. Dasher, what say you to three middies of Reschs?"

"Five quid, eh. That's a fortune for a squirt. You can get whatever you want as long as you've got a pocketful of spondulicks. Your old man and that prick in the blue suit took every penny I owned," Murray says.

"Yeah, well, you were stupid enough to put the bet on," Walter retorts. Murray smacks him across the face with the back of his hand. "Shut your fucking mouth, you piece of shit." The blow stuns Walter.

"You gutless fat bastard. I'll fight you," Walter says through bleeding lips, but Dasher pistons a punch into Walter's kidneys, knocking the wind out of him.

"Feisty cunt, eh?"

"A carbon copy of his old man. The bog Irish idiot is too stupid to stay down," says Murray.

"Is he the bloke that..." Dasher's voice trails off as Walter gulps for air.

"His son," says Murray.

"Is his father Mick Vaughan's mate?" Dasher asks.

"Yeah."

"You've got a right prize here." Dasher grabs a handful of Walter's hair.

The manager and bouncer haul Tony and Quentin away from the lavatory, hustle them to the door and throw them outside onto the footpath. Vomit drips from the corner of Quentin's mouth.

"Jeez, Tony, your hair's mussed up." Quentin manages a pallid smile. "What now?"

"Back to Darlington, I suppose, and tell Frankie what happened," says Tony.

"What do you reckon happened to the Bug? I'm not going back in there. Let's get a cab. How much dough have you got?" Quentin reaches for the wallet in his back pocket. Gone. Rummages his fob pocket. Empty.

"My wallet." Tony checks his pockets.

"Bastards rolled us."

"Then it's a bloody long walk." Tony places an arm around Quentin's shoulder, and joins the crowd lurching down William Street.

. . .

"Drink this, sport," Dasher says. Trembling, Walter puts the glass to his lips and gulps the meady ale, leans his head against the backrest and feels his muscles relax.

"You want to make fifty quid?" Dasher looks puzzled, but Walter turns a reddened face to Murray and asks, "Doing what"?

"It's amazing, Dasher. Doesn't matter how young, they perk up at the sound of money. What is the youth of our country coming to? All you've got to do is deliver a parcel to a bloke in Coogee."

Murray removes a fifty-pound note from his wallet, holds it to Walter's face, tears it in half, and places one portion on the table.

"You get the other half when you finish the job." Murray winks. Dasher flashes a knowing smile. Walter looks at the torn bill, reaches out his hand, and grasps the half.

. . .

The crowd dwindles into single male stragglers and couples. Quentin and Tony turn into a street near Walter's aunt's home. As the neon lights fade, the murky street appears more menacing than the energetic, pressing throng.

"How are we going to get home? Bloody miles from here." Tony props Quentin against a wall and sits next to him.

"I've got to get a drink of water."

"Sneak into a yard and use a tap."

"Maybe we can jump a tram to Pitt Street, and take it from there." Quentin stands and staggers toward a large, dun-coloured terraced house. A dim light flickers in a ground floor window.

…

Murray calls a waitress over to the booth.

"Get us a napkin, darling."

"Who's your young friend, Murray?" The waitress smiles at Walter, now feeling no pain.

"You gonna let him put his face in your bosom?" Dasher leers at the waitress.

"He's a damn sight better looking than you." The napkin sails on to Dasher's face and the woman flounces back to the bar.

Murray reaches into his pocket, places his closed fist inside the napkin, folds it and puts the package into his jacket.

"Let's go," he says, and the threesome walks to the rear entrance.

…

Quentin drinks water from the palm of his hand, and as he wipes droplets from his mouth, he looks into the face of the woman from the bistro.

"Well, if it isn't the boy with the gammy leg."

"Tony!"

"And your mates are here. Gavin will be so pleased."

"Oh no, not you," says Tony.

"Happy to see me? Good. Come inside. I insist."

"No thanks. We've got to be going," Tony says.

"Inside now, or I whistle up the dogs. You two are trespassing."

"He just wants a drink of water, lady. He's sick."

"Poor diddums. Come along. Gavin will brew a nice cup of tea to help settle the tum."

"A minute ago you said we were trespassing, and now you're inviting us inside," says Tony.

"Come along."

Set back from the road, a carriage path girdles the property perimeter. A copse of palm trees distinguishes the house as one of several, grand mid-nineteenth century mansions lining William Street. But now the estate stinks of decay, and reeks of piss. The dank grounds and creaking timber stairs smell of mushrooms.

A long hall disappears into blackness, save for a solitary light flickering at the far end of the corridor. An unseen cat hisses, and slinks into a hidden room. Tony beats the air around his face to remove fearful, clinging cobwebs.

Rosie, walking behind the two boys, calls "Gavin, put the kettle on will you? One of our dear warriors has a tummy upset, and is desperate for a cup of your lovely herbal tea."

"Whatever you wish, my dear." Gavin's modulated voice resonates from inside the house. Tony stops at the candle-lit doorway. "In you go," Rosie says, with a smile in her voice.

…

Walter sits between Dasher and Murray in the front seat of a black Holden. The car stops in a darkened, quiet suburban street. Surf booms in the distance.

"Up to the front door, nice and quiet, unwrap the napkin, put the parcel on the step, ring the bell, and back to the car. Simple. Do me this favour and the other half of the fifty is yours. If you don't, Dasher here plasters your nose across your fucking face, and don't try to do a runner."

"Which house?" Murray points to a dark red-brick Federation cottage, separated from the street by a low brick fence.

"Watch out for the dog."

"What dog?"

"You'll just have to be extra quiet. Go on. We'll wait here with the motor running." Murray hands Walter the napkin, now squeezed into a grimy ball. "Don't open it till you get to the door, and bring the bloody napkin back. Now piss off."

"I'm gonna shit myself," Walter whispers under his breath. "Get on with it," Murray hisses behind him.

Walter leaps the fence, and in a low crouch, moves toward a darkened window, avoiding the path. He squats behind a hydrangea, unties the napkin. A brass .303 bullet glints in his hand. Stuffing the napkin back in his pocket, Walter creeps toward the door, but dives onto the grass as a car passes in the street.

The sea thunders. Walter creeps on his haunches, places the bullet on the door mat, reaches for the bell and pushes the button, which triggers a quartet of chimes. Walter turns, runs and hurdles the fence, the sound of internal footsteps behind him.

"I've got it."

Light floods the porch. Walter leaps into the back seat, and peers out the rear window, and as the car speeds away, a tall man reaches down and picks up the bullet. Police Sergeant Mick Vaughan.

...

In William Street, a flickering candle stub sputters light throughout the room. A thin blue gas jet adds to the aura. Gavin stands over the sink, fills a kettle and motions the boys to sit.

"Cut off the electricity a week ago. I can cook as long as the gas is on, but when it's gone, we sup with Master Matthew Talbot Esquire, formerly of Dublin's Fair City. A poet's life, dear boys, is a poor existence. Rosie keeps body and soul together. Sells a few paintings, reads the odd palm, and meets the occasional British gent, don't you darling?"

"Don't be cruel, Gavin," but Rosie's tone is insincere.

"My dear, admit it. You are partial to pain." Gavin sits next to Tony and tousles his hair, but Tony pushes his hand away.

"Temper, temper, dear boy. Nothing to fear."

The kettle whistles on the stove and Gavin brews a small pot of strange smelling tea.

"Chamomile. It won't hurt your friend. Soothe his stomach. Sweeten it with honey." Gavin pushes the tea pot and a cracked cup toward Quentin. "It's good for you, I promise." Quentin fills his cup, stirs in a spoonful of honey and sips.

"Delicious."

"See. What did I tell you?"

"What a weird place," Tony says.

"It's our studio, but the police consider it a dive, and our drunken friends claim it as a squat. We've lived here for years." Gavin lifts his eyes from Quentin and stares at Rosie who whispers, "Would you like to see my paintings."

"Yes."

"Good. I admire a man with spirit."

"I'll come too," Tony says, but Gavin hisses, "Stay here."

...

"I'm gonna be sick." Dasher brakes quickly. Walter opens the car door, and retches into the gutter. The car speeds off once more, weaving toward Bondi. Dasher pulls over by the beach and laughs.

"I wonder if the big-time copper will enjoy his gift."

"He'll shit himself," says Murray, "and so will your old man." Murray pulls the other half of the note from his pocket.

"Here. Don't spend it all at the same time." Walter takes the crumpled bill, and stuffs it into his pocket.

"Now fuck off." Dasher pushes Walter away from the car. Murray unwinds the passenger window, and shouts, "You're in deep now, smart arse, so keep your fucking mouth closed because I know your address. See you again, cunt. Now piss off." The car tyres screech. Walter walks to a stop, hails a tram and shivers all the way to the city.

...

Gavin picks up a dog-eared book and begins to read: "*A worker in dark rooms of space moving along a bridge of royal hearts that turned to inward dances, take all that love and turmoil to their own.*"

"One of my lesser known literary attempts. Join me, dear boy." Gavin pours sweet Muscatel into a jam jar.

"No thanks," Tony says, as goose pimples rise on his arms.

"Are you a poet?" he asks.

"*The man is either crazy or he is a poet.* I am both mad, and a poet, and Rosie whom you met in the

Arabian Cafe is an artist. She paints my verse and the voices, which speak to her from across the astral plane."

Gavin lifts the flickering candle high above his head. Hot wax drips onto his wrist and hand, and as the light glimmers, a dim glow illuminates charcoal drawings of winged serpents with elongated tongues and devilish bat faces. Naked women with Rosie's features, copulate with serpents and tumescent dogs. Tony whimpers. Gavin lowers the candle and pushes the beaker of wine toward him.

"Drink. Hell will never be full till you enter."

Tony takes the jar, but throws the wine at Gavin, and bellowing, runs to the door. Gavin laughs, and licks the streams of Muscatel dripping down his face.

"A boy is a cross between a god and a goat," he shouts, and drains his tumbler.

"Feeling better?" Rosie sounds sympathetic.

"Do you really have a crystal ball?"

"Are you curious?"

"What will I see?"

"You must decide." Rosie walks ahead of Quentin and up the stairs. "Careful. In here," she says, and disappears into a blackened room.

A match scrapes. A candle sputters.

"Come in," she says. The room reeks of stale linen and paint. An iron bedstead stands beneath a window. Rosie pushes clothes on to the floor, straightens the covers and motions Quentin to sit.

"Beware of my pet spiders." She laughs as Quentin brushes the bed. "Now where did I put the crystal," she says, rummaging in the gloom.

"Here it is. I must prepare before a reading." Rosie unfastens a clip, and the cloak falls away, revealing a plain, blue smock stained with paint, which she pulls over her head.

"Am I attractive?"

"Yes."

"Look." Rosie raises her left arm. A web of pink tissue stretching from arm pit to elbow, slowly unfolds. Rosie gently massages her body, and begins to utter words Quentin does not understand. He reaches out to touch the bat wing, but Rosie playfully tut tuts. "You have much to learn about women, my dear." Tony's yelping breaks the mood. Quentin jumps off the bed, runs out the door and down the stairs.

"Bastard." Rosie screams at the fleeing Quentin, and begins to whistle. Both boys collide, shout in fright, and run toward the front door.

A dog yaps in the darkness. Cats hiss and spit as Gavin's laughter fills the vacant rooms. Rosie screeches at the top of her voice, whistling up unseen dogs.

Quentin and Tony chase a toast rack tram trundling William Street, grab the handrails, and jump the footboard. Kings Cross disappears.

Adrenalin thwarts sleep. Quentin and Tony talk till dawn in the front room of the Moroney house. Walter arrives an hour or so after his friends, and the three describe the events of the night. Bravado replaces fear.

"How'd you get the black eye?"

"A fight."

"Didya win?"

"Did I ever?" Walter pulls out the halves of the fifty pound note. "Got this for my trouble."

"Fair dinkum. Who did you fight?" Quentin asks.

"No one much. What happened to you guys?"

"You'll never guess who we ran into. The beatniks from the cafe," Tony says.

"Dead set. What happened?"

"The bloke tried to crack on to me, and Quentin went upstairs with the sheila."

"Pull the other one, Gallagher."

"I did. Fair dinkum. She stripped off. You should've seen it."

"You and Gavin. Bit suss, Tony."

"Get out of it. Nothing happened. I ran. You should have seen the paintings in the room. Bloody devils. They're lunatics."

"So, did you do it?" Walter asks Quentin.

"This cove yelled out so bloody loud, I nearly jumped out of my skin. We bolted."

"Top night," Quentin says.

"I'm never going back to the Cross." Tony is solemn.

"And you Bug?"

"Who knows?"

Anthony (Tony) Moroney won a bursary to Sydney University. To mark this achievement his name is engraved in gold on the St Gloria's honour role. Tony studied law, passed the entire bar exams, married and reared three children. He won pre-selection to contest a seat for the Australian Labor Party, and served several distinguished terms in the New South Wales Parliament.

Quentin Gallagher became indentured to a master horse trainer, and to this day manages racing stables for a thoroughbred syndicate. He is a well-known racing industry identity.

Rosie and Gavin collaborated with the great British conductor Sir Eugene Goosens on a musical version of *The Fall of the House of Usher*, an ironic collusion which culminated in a scandal which destroyed Goosens' distinguished career. Rosie died quietly in the Sacred Heart Hospice, Darlinghurst. Gavin Greenlees passed away in a small apartment on the fourth anniversary of Rosie's death. His poetry is ignored by Sydney's literary cognoscenti, and while the remnants of the occult painting of his beloved are dismissed by the Sydney art world, Rosie – Rosaleen – Norton is remembered as the Witch of Kings Cross.

Dazzled by bright lights, Walter Sugden swapped football for boxing, and fought on a dozen low-ranking cards as a semi-professional at the Sydney Stadium in Rushcutters Bay.

# Chapter Seventeen
## Best and Fairest

Family and friends walked to Central Railway Station to bid Declan goodbye. Aunt Maude packed a blanket, a thermos of tea and a box of Devon sandwiches as Jimmy prowled the length of the platform looking for an empty compartment.

The journey to Walgett took twelve hours. Declan's excitement abated after the city environs fell away. Snatches of fitful sleep on a hard green leather bench, punctuated the boredom and rattling torpor.

A posse of children greeted Declan at the Walgett wheat terminal the following morning. His father, after whom Declan was named, stood in the background, smiling faintly at the hubbub erupting around his son.

Declan kissed the woman he now knew to be his mother, a younger, mirror image of Aunt Maude.

The Walgett Warriors turned out to be a team of sharpies, and the relative from Sydney agreed to stay an extra week, but a terse telegram from Uncle Jimmy saying "get back for training or else" cut the visit short.

The Darlington fourteens shot ahead in the schools competition, and a re-run of last year's grand final seemed a certainty, but the year-long grind of training and weekend games took a toll. Tempers flared over a loss, while a win seemed devoid of lustre, yet despite the interminable round of matches, Jimmy's rigorous discipline managed to keep the players focussed.

Ken muscled up and resembled his father in physique. Cyril proved a wily hooker as Neil and Tony held the formation firm. When Enzo packed down, an opposing scrum stood no chance of a twist off the mark. Quentin, master of the second row feed, when caught by the referee, invariably responded with an "aww, sir." Walter remained play-maker extraordinaire and game pivot at five eighth. Mark remained calm at inside centre, and his brother Peter Tregonning flighty on his outside. Fullback Chris remained cool and deadly in defence, prowling the rear of play, alive to every chance, and safe as houses under spiralling high punts. But the uncanny skill of the wingers brought parents and supporters to every game. Billy found the spot when the playmaker called, and flash Declan remained as ever, wry, swift, and unpredictable. As captain, Walter watched the group develop with trepidation. As each player matured to a level of skill equivalent to or greater than his own, his authority diminished, especially when Quentin and Vice-captain Chris openly questioned his role as chief play-maker.

This year no individual stood out, as had happened in the previous season. For the first time in his life, Walter yearned for more than sporting plaudits. Money. The repaired torn fifty pound note financed a new pair of football boots, an occasional tip for a taxi driver, and a year's subscription to *Rugby League Week*.

His scant earnings ceased with the end of the paper run, and the loss of the pocket money made Walter pay attention to his father's obsessive rants about filthy lucre. As a gambler who eked a living as an illegal bookmaker, Frankie proved hopeless with money. Walter's mother hid an assortment of pound notes to ensure the old man didn't punt the rent, or the school fees. But as enthusiasm for schoolboy football waned, Walter's ability in the ring flourished. Murray Dwyer and Dasher Doug Morgan turned up at the Darlington Police Boys Club on the night Walter fought for a junior crown. Jimmy Bomer and Mick Vaughan worked his corner, while the under fourteens' team barracked from the bleachers. Walter's parents stayed away; Frankie too drunk and his mother terrified of seeing her son beaten to pulp. Murray, always on the make, organised a bet on Walter, who won the three-round fight on a technical knockout. Walter found an envelope in his cabinet in the locker room. A scrawled note, wrapped in a five pound bill read "meet me," an address in Kings Cross, and a date and time.

Walter began missing training sessions, and late in the season skipped games altogether. During the turmoil Chris acted as captain, and Jimmy offered Vince Vansittart a run as five eighth. When Walter eventually showed up for training or a game, he appeared listless and irritable. As the season came to an end, Jimmy became convinced the behaviour of his wayward skipper would lose the competition. Jimmy mentioned his concerns to Frankie who promised to belt sense into his son. But Walter refused to stay home, and Frankie chose to concentrate his sober moments on the upcoming Sydney Spring

Carnival, a racing event deemed more important than his son's future.

The semi-final games were split between city and country schools, and for the first time in history, Walgett made a failed attempt at the championship. Thus, with one game to go, a replay of last year's thriller loomed between Darlington and old rival Bankstown.

A fortnight before the grand final, parents, friends and supporters crowded the St Gloria's auditorium for speech night. The school principal handed out keepsakes to junior champions, and awarded larger trophies to the seniors. Of all the school teams and individual players, only the under fourteens reached the championship round.

Best and Fairest loomed as the premier accolade of the year. A contender had to demonstrate superlative skill, and a mature, constructive attitude toward teammates, opponents and officials, both on and off field.

Enzo thought himself a chance, but won most improved player for the second year in a row. Chris became an outside tip for the award, but the audience felt confident the distinction would go to the Bug.

Declan Bennet walked away with the gold cup. Gasps and murmurs of "Abo bastard," greeted the announcement, but in a unanimous decision the judging panel declared Declan had proved his worth throughout the season. Despite being aware of the reasons why his son had lost the tribute, Frankie stormed out of the auditorium, but Walter stood and applauded Declan as Jimmy, Billy and Maude beamed with pride.

By week's end, Declan vanished. Only Billy knew where he had gone, and Jimmy threatened him with a backhander when he refused to reveal Declan's whereabouts.

Declan told Billy he felt homesick, and on the Friday night jumped a train to Walgett to play with the Warriors in the Koori Knockout. The Warriors lost. On the Sunday night return trip to Sydney, two policemen questioned Declan, and demanded identity papers. Declan's soiled football gear convinced the police of his excuse. When realising Declan's age the coppers let him go with a warning, and a gob full of racist insults. The incident was the first of a lifetime of run-ins with the law.

Word went out again to Vince Vansittart to substitute on the wing, and the Darlington fourteens cruised to an easy win over a Newtown school, in the second semi-final. Chris Robertson's unerring boot put the game out of doubt, in more ways than anybody realised at the time.

The victory meant a grand final between Darlington and Bankstown, with the winners touring England with the Kangaroo squad. A count back decided the choice of venue for the grand final. The team with the highest points rate nominated the ground. Chris's goal in the preceding game gave Darlington the choice and with the margin, Jimmy Bomer selected the home ground of Henson Park, a hard oval for a tough match.

Declan's award, his subsequent absence, and Walter's erratic form, disrupted the pre-match routine. Team cohesion disintegrated. Declan snapped at his mates. Walter's indifference worried the coach. Cyril fretted over an external exam for an Army apprenticeship, and Quentin's year-long growth spurt exacerbated his embarrassment with the deficiency of his leg. Puffy-faced and bruised, Mark and Peter Tregonning endured their father's brutality while John Flood savoured the pangs of first love.

The remainder – Chris, Terry, Enzo, Billy, Ken and Neil – weathered the turmoil as best they could, but the Darlington under fourteen all stars seemed to have little chance of beating Bankstown.

The grand final ended in a fourteen point draw. The referee allocated forty minutes extra time, but the deadlock remained unbroken. Coaches from both teams demanded the New South Wales Rugby League settle the matter. Travel arrangements had been made for the winners, and names required for the airline manifest. Opposing school headmasters held an emergency meeting with football officials and St Gloria's Darlington scored the win, again on a countback.

The meeting ended in acrimony, and by the following morning the story headlined the Sydney tabloid sports pages. A Rugby League development officer solved the imbroglio, suggesting both teams worthy of the State Championship and the England tour, but only fourteen players, including a reserve, could travel. The officer recommended a ballot. Seven players chosen from Darlington, because of the all stars position as official winners, and six from Bankstown, with a reserve selected on the toss of a coin. Neil Davidson, Tony Moroney, Paul Tregonning, Billy Bomer, John Flood, Enzo Cuda and Chris Robertson made the trip to the passport office. The coin toss eliminated Vince Vansittart, and the secret ballot had excluded Declan. The remaining team members accepted green and gold blazers, long grey trousers, a football, a trophy and a framed team photograph.

But the team, assembled by the coin toss, existed in name only. Confusion about who played what position and no time for training proved catastrophic. The hybrid group touring with the Kangaroos lost every match to their England schoolboy opponents. The football year ended in debacle.

Of the thirteen under fourteen Darlington players, two graduated to the professional league. Declan passed an undistinguished career with the Newtown Blue Bags. Cousin Billy played with the South Sydney Rabbitohs before a severe hamstring injury forced an early retirement.

William (Billy) Bomer is a respected coach with a major Queensland Rugby League club.

Despite the accolade of Best and Fairest, cigarettes, alcohol, time served in prison, and chronic diabetes, shortened Declan Bennett's life to 38 years.

# Chapter Eighteen
# Theosophy

Enzo spoke Italian with a broad Australian accent. His grandparents barely understood their gigantic offspring, while Enzo found it difficult to comprehend his elders' rich dialect. But on Sunday afternoons at raucous gatherings in a large house on Australia Street, Newtown, family and friends rekindled memories of life in Santa Croce, Florence, the city of Enzo's birth.

Emigrant students at St Gloria's endured the humiliating taunts of "wog" and "dago", epithets rarely directed at Enzo. Height and build spared him the insults, and his increasing skills demanded genuine respect. Not once during his years at "glows" did Enzo reveal the rich history of football played by his father and uncles, a brutal brawl Florentines call *calico storico*.

Much as Enzo admired the footballers who adorned the player cards, he idolised motor cars; not the chunky Fords and snub-nosed FJ Holden utes trundling the alleys of Paddy's Markets, but the sleek, stylish, Ferraris, Lamborghinis and Maseratis, whose pictures adorned his bedroom wall.

In his fourteenth year Enzo chose to become a draftsman, and return to Italy to serve an apprenticeship in a small motor shop owned by an uncle. In the month Enzo boarded the M.S. *Achille Lauro*, the bugaboo of conscription passed the Australian Senate. The sojourn meant Enzo avoided the likelihood of fighting in a little-known country called Vietnam.

The under fourteen year prompted Enzo's friend Cyril Smyth to make a life altering choice. The Australian Army offered apprenticeships in Victoria. A suitable pass in science and mathematics in the Intermediate Certificate meant a welcome for most candidates. Advertisements for the scholarships, worth five thousand pounds, appeared in the *Daily Mirror*. Cyril wrote the telephone number of the Combined Services Recruiting Centre on the back of his maths text book.

During their schoolboy football career, Enzo and Cyril developed an uncanny understanding of each other's skills. Talent scouts from Newtown attempted to coax them to join the junior ranks. Both declined.

Cyril, the only child of aged parents, relished the rough camaraderie of school life. Unlike the majority of his classmates who lived within walking distance, Cyril called a large decrepit house in a narrow street behind Newington College, home.

An ancestor on his father's side of the family accompanied Blaxland, Lawson and Wentworth across the eucalyptus and sandstone barrier of the Blue Mountains, and the early Victorian mansion in Stanmore comprised the patrilineal legacy of Cyril's father Roger Smyth.

The Great Depression withered the house to a weedy wasteland. A talent as a classical organist and belief in Theosophy granted Roger entry to a formidable cabal of the rich and the reckless, many of whom had trod the nine circles of hell in the War to End all Wars.

Roger played organ for poets and philosophers at vegetarian banquets held in the Commonwealth Club on Elizabeth Street. He discussed architecture with Walter Burley Griffin, and fell in love with Marion Burley Griffin's best friend, Kylie Laurence. Marion and Kylie swore they would never bring children into a world where, on the eve of battle, wizened generals prayed for the death of a mere ten thousand men.

Yet Marion Burley Griffin yearned for a child, and told friends at a stylish soiree of her practice of leaving a box of apples at the front gate of her Castlecrag home. An apple stolen by a child she said, tasted sweeter.

Marion and Walter Burley Griffin, Kylie, Roger and sundry devotees of Theosophy believed a new messiah walked the Earth, a sadhu trained since childhood by Madame Helena Blavatsky. This new Christ, Kylie said, was Jiddu Krishnamurti. She and hundreds of believers built a grand rotunda on the Mosman foreshore to witness the Indian saviour's miraculous entry to Sydney, atop the foaming waters off the Heads. But the touted utopia wilted beneath the heat of endless summers of Depression, and Kylie's dream of an ennobled world shrank to the paltry light of a solitary candle, and the poetry of Judith Wright which she read aloud as her husband played J.S. Bach's *Trio Sonatas*.

Pregnancy came as an unwanted surprise, yet her mild, ginger-headed son caused no trouble throughout infancy. The onset of post-natal osteoarthritis dazed the porcelain beauty into a stupor of forgetfulness. The sedate Cyril played amid books stacked floor to ceiling, many written by his parents' acquaintances of the Lost Generation.

Football became a constant of Cyril's teen years. He enjoyed the regimentation, the friendship, the training and discipline. Football made him feel part of a cohesive unit.

Enzo befriended Cyril and welcomed him into the tumult of an extended family that laughed and argued and ate and drank wine as freely as they kissed one another.

Enzo's father Niccolo, who spoke no English, regaled the assembly with stories of Romulus and Remus, and the Sacred Geese. The mystery of the tattered Shroud of Turin enthralled Cyril. Enzo translated and embellished his father's colloquy.

Both youths passed idle time discussing their future. Cyril avoided mentioning his parents, describing his father as retired, and saying his mother was ill, but Enzo told rambling stories about the deeds of innumerable relatives. A well-to-do uncle living in a crumbling Roman villa had invited young Enzo to visit the Eternal City. One long, summer stay, Enzo and his sisters enjoyed the freedom of the small estate, where they played for hours amid ruined, classical statuary. During a game of hide and seek, Enzo searched a remote corner of the domain, rank with rotting vegetation and wild grape vine. Tinkling water lured him to dark underbrush where, on hands and knees, he crawled toward a diminutive, forgotten grotto. Willow fronds filtered dappled sunlight on a figure the size of an infant. Enzo strained to look at the face of the idol, and as a breath of wind parted the tendrils, a shaft of light illuminated the hideous, grimacing visage of an ancient Etruscan deity. So powerful the shock, Enzo said, he stood amid the briars, tearing through the tangle, emerging into the garden, bloodied by thorns, screaming in terror.

Enzo described culture beyond the red brick monotony of St Gloria's. His eloquent visions filled Cyril's threadbare nights with dreams of fabled lands. Their fellowship prompted Cyril to apply for the apprenticeship. In the year following the under fourteen's ambiguous football triumph, Cyril swapped his loveless Stanmore home for the freezing barracks of the Australian Army Apprentices training ground near Mornington in Victoria.

For Cyril the window of the world opened on a strange land. He boarded the HMAS *Melbourne*, along with hundreds of Australian soldiers, en route to a base camp near the port village of Vung Tau, in the Vietnamese province of Phuoc Tui.

Cyril crossed and recrossed the Timor Sea four times during the Vietnam War, and slept aboard the night the old aircraft carrier sliced the HMAS *Voyager* in half, miles off the emerald coast of Jervis Bay. Cyril did not know the father of his former team mate, Neil Davidson, helped build the *Voyager*.

It may be natural to celebrate the serendipitous, and forget the calamitous, but Lance Corporal Smyth could not blot out his experiences in the dank Vietnamese jungles.

Cyril demobilised into a hostile Australia, and during a khaki life which took him to Nui Dat and Long Tan, Cyril's fellow citizens campaigned for and won profound change at home.

Although skilled in military trades, Cyril lost his way in a land of hippies. He drifted into a job with a film company, working as a stage hand, and production assistant building landscapes of make believe; cardboard realms that provided momentary escape from recollections of the horrors of combat.

Cyril lodged in collective households, and drove a Triumph Tiger motorbike to film shoots. After absences of days or weeks on location, Cyril pushed the motorbike into the lounge room, stripped and rebuilt the motor, and took it apart again.

Cyril could not sleep, and when fatigue pushed him to unconsciousness, his eyes remained open. He now lives in a four-wheel-drive car, and tows a battered caravan around outback Australia.

Enzo chases the good life, financed by a fortune earned as a motor car designer. Each summer he entertains family in a sumptuous house in Ischia. When the season ends, Enzo indulges his passion for motor racing, before returning to Sydney to pass the bleak months of the northern winter in a tasteful bungalow in Haberfield.

Enzo considered forming a Rugby League club in his home town, but Florentines preferred Rugby Union, especially after Rugby Union legend David Campese toured their city.

One day over coffee and biscotti in a bistro on Ramsay Street, Enzo told me he had neither seen nor heard from Cyril since the year the Darlington under fourteen all stars won the state championships. It is improbable they will meet again.

# Chapter Nineteen
# The Snarler

A churning sea batters the coast, sending salt spray inland toward the city. A sleek, imported Chevrolet sits in front of a squat brick house. A sharp-featured young man fidgets at the steering wheel. Sheet lightning crackles static, breaking the sonority of Chick Henderson's rendition of *Begin the Beguine.*

Nothing had changed since the last visit; the low brick fence, the blue hydrangeas in a line along the neat path to the door, the trimmed hedge beneath the bedroom windows. But the old fear returned with the memory of the chill feel of lead and the dim glimmer of the brass casing of the World War One .303 bullet.

"Too bloody big," he says under his breath, but words fail to calm a jangle of nerves.

"I needed this baby." He pops the lock on the glove box and grasps a grey snub-nosed .38 pistol, unfastens the safety latch, clicks the tumbler, spins the chamber and snaps it shut. A coating of oil mingles with sweat on his palm.

"I'll dump it when the job's done, and nick another one," he whispers as the bolero syncopates to the stroke of the arc of windscreen wipers.

"Coppers are bastards. I hate 'em. Pay 'em off, and they're back for more. Bugger them. I don't give a stuff. A bet is a bet. That's the way it goes. You play, you pay. Come on. I can't sit here for eternity."

A porch light blinks and a flip of a switch silences the radio. The wiper stops with a click. He cocks the hammer, but mist clouds the windscreen.

"Fuck."

Flick.

The wiper motor screeches.

Mick Vaughan peers through the haze at the parked car, and slips into a darkened room, deep in the house.

Click. The porch darkens.

"Shit."

Mick strides toward the car, pumping a shotgun. The young man grabs the door handle. Locked. Grasps the car door lock, but oil and sweat slither his hand. Frantic winds on the window handle.

He elevates the .38 to chest level.

Surf thunders.

Exploding shotgun slugs pulverise glass.

"Silly prick." Mick pulls on the door latch, opens the smoking, blood-spattered vehicle. The smashed body slumps onto wet tar.

The quiet Coogee roadway fills with detectives and ambulances. Television cameramen and reporters push against blue police tape. Rain washes blood the length of the gutter. The reek of burnt flesh and cordite mingle in the salt-mist air. A young constable drapes an old coverlet over the corpse. Neighbours stand in doorways. Sirens wail. Mick walks toward his house. A detective shouts, "Bomber's here."

"Show him in."

"What's this bloody mess, Vaughan? It's as bad as Kings Cross on a Saturday night. Who's the fucking snarler?" The senior detective removes his pork pie hat, places it on the sideboard.

"Walter Sugden. Murray Dwyer's enforcer. Minor hood. His old man runs a Starting Price tote in Darlington. His dad is a good mate. We go back a while." The senior detective raises an eyebrow.

"Sugden. Ex Newtown Blue Bags' junior?"

"No," Mick says, "but he showed promise when he was a kid. Did a bit of amateur boxing. Went a couple of rounds as a professional. I trained him. Had the makings of a tasty bantamweight, but dropped out of sight and, eh," Mick sighs, "teamed up with our old mate."

"So why did he come around with a lead calling card, Mick? Old times or something more important?" Mick grimaces at Bomber's humour.

"Misunderstanding over money."

"Dead fucking set. Isn't it always the case," Bomber says.

"So Murray Dwyer's involved in this mess right up his fucking neck to his mouth."

"Got it in one." Mick paces the room, and peeps through the curtains at the mayhem.

"Took a while for Murray to learn the ropes, but he's got the gift now for sure. Remember the barney he got into a few years ago with the sharpie in the blue suit, what's his name?" Bomber reaches for a pack of cigarettes.

"The Ringer. Fucking twerp from Queensland."

"The very same. Frankie Sugden and the Ringer skinned Murray on a mug's bet at 100 to 1. I was working the Slasher case at the time.

Murray came whinging for a favour. The idiot, gambled the lot, and the Ringer walked away laughing. Took him for every skerrick he owned. But his luck changed when he met up with Dasher Doug Morgan."

"If memory serves me, Dasher is a slash artist. Ran with Guido Culetti in Woolloomooloo back in the thirties. Razor scar across his cheek?"

Mick nods. "Morgan and Dwyer start a stand-over business in the Cross – tiny town hoons smacking working girls in the kidneys. Then Dwyer starts winning big on Fan Tan, and puts this young snarler on the payroll as his debt collector in the opium dens.

"Frankie didn't know his son joined up with Dwyer and Morgan. He took a commission from the original mugs bet, and went on with the S.P. He hates Dwyer, and for the life of me I never figured out why."

"Might be because Dwyer's in the brotherhood." Bomber pours a double brandy.

"Are you telling me Murray Dwyer is a Freemason?"

"Bet your life, Mick," Bomber says, and begins whistling the tune, *the sash my father wore.*

"Well, fuck me fuckin' ragged," Mick says.

"Fuck you is right, Mick. You just fucking killed your best mate's son."

"Him or me."

"Fair enough. No worries mate. I'll have a word in Macquarie Street. Tell you what. Take a few weeks off. The bream will be on the bite on the South Coast when this bloody storm blows out. I'll call you when the heat's off, but you might be posted over to the North Shore." Bomber winks toward Mick, and bangs his glass on the table.

"What happens to Frankie Sugden?"

"He'll read all about it in the papers."

"Tough call," Mick says.

"Don't front him. Stay away," Bomber says, glaring at Mick. "How much are you into Dwyer for?"

"Four thousand."

"Can you cover it?"

"Me and the boys were working on a plan before the kid showed up," Mick says.

"Dead for four thousand quid, eh? Hardly worth it. Remember those three monkeys, Mick, me old son. Hear no evil, see no evil, and as for speaking no evil, I'll brief this lot of slavering, fucking monkeys."

The senior detective retraces his steps along the hall, and walks into a starburst of lights. A scrum of journalists fire questions, but the Bomber brushes them aside.

"Come to CIB headquarters tomorrow morning for a full statement," he says, and strolls toward a dark American Ford Fairlane. A blue illuminated crown with the word Police sits atop the roof. Bomber is Sydney's top cop.

Coroner's men dressed in rubber overalls roll the body onto a black plastic sheet, haul the zippered bag onto a stretcher, and place it in a slot in the rear of a black van. Police photographers film the scene. A detective places the .38 pistol into a plastic evidence bag. Journalists in raincoats question ambulance drivers. A fireman hoses the gutter, and spreads buckets of sand across gobs of blood and gore on the grass. A tow truck driver winches the Chevy onto the back of a lorry, and drives behind a police escort car. Flashing red and blue lights dim and fade. Yawning neighbours shut their doors. Unseen bullfrogs croak in the wet. Surf pounds Wedding Cake Island. Mick pours brandy and calls to his mates.

"So what do we do about Dwyer?" one of the men asks.

"He'll keep," but Mick's hands shake and the brandy spills onto the carpet.

"Tell you what that fucking hoodlum's problem was," he says to no one in particular.

"Me. I never miss. That bastard Dwyer sent a boy to do a man's job. Set him up. We knew there'd be heavies, but..." Mick's voice quavers and his words trail into silence.

"How could you know Murray would send the kid? We'll straighten him out later."

"No, we won't. Murray's got the best kind of protection going." Mick pours more brandy and peers out the window onto the dark street. "It's going to be a long night, and for the first time in my life, I'm going to get drunk."

# Chapter Twenty
## Sugar

Chris Robertson eases a steel letter opener beneath the flap of a Manilla envelope, runs the blunt edge the length of the sleeve, reaches inside and removes a sheaf of leaflets.

"Another appeal," he says aloud, and places the handbill inside a battered leather brief case.

"Are you there?" Three swift knocks on the door follow the call of a gruff voice.

"Come in. I'll make a pot of tea."

Chris fills an old blackened kettle, clatters cups onto saucers, takes milk from the fridge, and a canister of sugar from a shelf.

"Take a seat." Chris motions, but the tradesman prefers to stand. Dried white paint smatters every square inch of the housepainter's overalls, blending with a cotton cap that hides a receding pate.

"My partner's coming later this afternoon. It's tough getting a job this size these days, Chris. I appreciate it, mate. Money's tight."

"Money." says Chris. "Everybody puts out their hand. I'm no exception. I spend all my time maintaining this bloody old school." Chris pours milk into his cup, spoons two measures and stirs the brew.

"I visited France when I was fourteen. Boarded for six weeks with an elderly uncle who fought in World War One."

"How did you wind up in France at that age?" The painter stirs three teaspoons into the steaming tea.

"Toured England with the Kangaroos as part of a schoolboy outfit. There are a couple of photographs of me along the hall, near the entrance to the auditorium. Long time ago now. My uncle and aunt paid my fare across the English Channel. They lived in a small village close to Fromelles, near the Belgian border. He was blinded by German mustard gas, and my aunt nursed him after the big battle. They married and farmed a few head of cattle.

"One weekend we caught the train to Paris, to visit the Cathedral of St Denis, built by an abbott named Sugar. Started building the church in the eleventh[h] century. I've never seen anything as magnificent in my life. I've got an old history guide somewhere," Chris says, and walks into a study. After a few minutes rummaging, he returns with a battered volume, clears his throat and reads aloud.

*Thus, when out of my delight in the beauty of the House of God the loveliness of the many coloured gems has called me away from external cares, and worthy meditation has induced me to reflect, transferring that which is material to that which is immaterial, on the diversity of the sacred virtues; then it seems to me that I see myself dwelling, as it were, in some strange region which exists neither in the slime of the earth nor entirely in the purity of heaven; and that, by the grace of God, I can be transported from this inferior to the higher world.*

The housepainter squirms in the chair. "I didn't understand a word, Chris."

"I went to school here, and now I'm the fulltime caretaker. For better or worse, this is my monument. When you and your mate do the painting, or a bit of carpentry, perhaps you'll become part of the legacy. You can't tell me you do this just for money?"

The housepainter bangs the cup onto the saucer, stands and walks to the door. "Pardon me, Chris, but what the fuck else do I work for? Thanks for the tea and, eh, I'd appreciate if you settle up when we finish."

# Chapter Twenty One
# Rabbitoh

A whistle rouses an old man from a light sleep.

"Pension day." he mutters. "Get the paper. Pass the time. Might pick a winner, or meet up with mates for a yarn."

Cars and trucks roar past the front door.

"Everyone's in a hurry. No time to stop for a chat. Takes a friggin' year to get out of bed. Remember when mum baked scones? So hot when they came out of the oven, they burnt your fingers, and the butter melted in yellow streams. Tough as an old hen, and just as cranky, weren't you, mum."

*Nothing better than a soft-boiled egg with salt; a slice of damper and a mug of tea. Cut the damper into strips, and dip the crust into the warm, soft yolk. Pullets are the best layers. You get a golden yolk every time. When you finish breakfast, go and feed the cabbage scraps to the chooks, and let 'em scratch around in the dirt, Frankie.*

"They're vicious bastards, mum. They peck one another, and have a go at me."

A chiming grandfather clock greets the afternoon.

"A few hours in the pub, eh? Open day and night these days. Can't drink as much as I used to. Bloody knees ache. Nothing in the papers. Load of rubbish. Sit and rest your eyes, old son. Near blind as a fruit bat now, but I could pop a bunny on the hop at a hundred yards, back in the day. A .303 cartridge was worth more than the rabbit, and if I didn't bag a dozen, the old man chased me and my brother around the yard hurling his belt above his head."

*Get us a string of bunnies to sell and a couple for tea. Make sure you get carrots and parsnips, and a bay leaf. Get on with it, Frankie.*

"Call it what you want—lunch, dinner, tea— doesn't make a damn bit of difference these days."

*Dad. Show us how you gut a rabbit.*

"The old man sharpened his bayonet on a whetstone, picked up a fat one, nicked it at the belly button, and peeled off the pelt as if a dainty glove then turned it inside out."

*The old lady'll sew this onto the baby's bunny rug.*

"My brother's eyes near popped when he slit the blue sinew from the flesh, gutted the cavity, and dropped the lot into the slop bucket."

*How come there's no blood?*

*Because I didn't puncture the heart, or liver. See? Clean flesh, and no fluke worm. Feed this lot to the dogs, Frankie.*

"Yeah, right oh."

"I can smell the gravy bubbling round the braising bunny. Mum shredded the hot flesh off the bones into the Dutch oven, and the old man dribbled spit into the stew. Laugh or what?"

*Next time get a friggin' dozen, and fucking vegies, or I'll wallop the both of you.*

"The Scarlet Fever killed my sister. Mum wrapped her in the bunny rug, and dad dug her grave at the back of the church in Warialda. Her coffin was barely the length of my arm. My uncle, I don't remember his name, filled a jam jar with honey and placed it in on top of the cairn. We couldn't afford a headstone."

The September afternoon slips away, and as the man droops forward, a warbling currawong mocks the traffic din. He wakes with a start, stands unsteady, but with the aid of a walking frame, pulls upright and shuffles toward the front door. Young men and women dressed in lycra shorts and shirts, jog along the road. A frayed belt secures a pair of baggy trousers high above a skinny rib cage. A fawn cardigan covers a faded, striped pyjama top. Creased yellow heels flip flop out of cheap slippers.

"Need whiskey to warm me."

The reek of commercial disinfectant fills the air before the cool, dim hotel comes into sight. Blinking poker machines squawk the length of the interior. A raspy male voice calls a football game from a wall-mounted colour television. Young men follow the match in silence, and then cheers spike the gloom. A man orders a round of drinks as a friend punches the air, walks toward a computer, and feeds a ticket into a slot.

The rusty frame nudges open the hotel door, and as the old man shuffles to the bar, a patron places a stool behind and eases him on to the seat.

"There you go, pops."

"Got a smoke?"

"You ought to give 'em a miss, grandad."

"Can't afford the bloody things these days," he says. A sloughing laugh morphs into a deep, bronchial cough.

A sharp whistle from the television splits the hubbub. "Who's playing?" he asks, but the din drowns out the response.

"Never heard of 'em," he scowls, and wheezes with each drag on the cadged cigarette.

"Me and my brother picked blackberries by the bagful out near Regents Park. Dry, dusty paddocks in those days. Just a mob of poor-arsed returned soldiers. Every one of 'em mad as cut snakes from the war. Ex-clerks and mechanics, and not a fucking farmer among them. Kidding themselves. Canterbury was a pretty spot though. Sweet smelling orange trees planted in rows along the rolling hills. Everybody owned a horse. The locals pushed and pushed for a race track. In the end they got what they wanted, but lost the trees. Close knit lot the Berries; always have been. I reckon they're the same today. Thick as thieves over in Newtown as well, eh. Why they ever got rid of the Blue Bags I'll never know. The game isn't the same. Why punish club supporters? League's buggered in the inner city. Different game from my day. No juniors around here anymore."

A boy wearing a backward-facing baseball cap opens the hotel door, releases the handle of a yellow pushcart filled with newspapers, bundles a dozen tabloids beneath an arm and calls "paper." Older drinkers tally small change off the bar into the boy's hand.

A waiter dressed in white shirt and black trousers stares at the man's unshaven face, and nicotine-stained fingers.

"What'll you have?"

"Whiskey. Water. No ice."

"Yep," he says, spins on his heel and selects a cheap bottle. Pours a nip into a shot glass, reaches for a water jug and tumbler, puts each item within reach, plucks a ten dollar note from the man's grasp, and drops the change into his fist.

"Howzat, pops?"

"I've lived here all my life," but the barman does not reply. "And I recall everything except being born. You remember mum? Don't reckon I'll know the moment I die, either."

"Paper, mister?" The voice startles the old man. Untrimmed, grey bushy eyebrows arch high on his face as the coins slip from his grasp, and fall soundless onto the beer damp carpet.

Now that you have finished reading *Best and Fairest*, Valentine Press and Henry Johnston would appreciate your feedback.

There is a Reader's Comments page for *Best and Fairest* on the Valentine Press website.